DEATH OR BOUNTY

DEATH OR BOUNTY

by

I. J. Parnham

Dales Large Print Books
Long Preston, North Yorkshire,
BD23 4ND, England.

British Library Cataloguing in Publication Data.

Parnham, I. J.
Death or bounty.

A catalogue record of this book is
available from the British Library

ISBN 1-84262-241-2 pbk

First published in Great Britain in 2002 by Robert Hale Limited

Published in Large Print 2003 by arrangement with
Robert Hale Limited

Dales Large Print is an imprint of Library Magna Books Ltd.

Printed and bound in Great Britain by
T.J. (International) Ltd., Cornwall, PL28 8RW

1

'Another delay,' Clifford Trantor muttered over the train's squealing brakes. He glared through the carriage window at the swirling fog outside. 'At this rate, we ain't ever reaching Beaver Ridge.'

As the train shuddered to a halt, he turned to the tall, rugged man sitting opposite to him, Bill Squires, who also stared through the window.

'Reckon as this fog is the worst I've seen,' Bill said.

Clifford nodded. 'Ain't surprising that we're making poor time, but that still don't make it all right.'

'Guessing as you're in a hurry to reach Beaver Ridge?'

'Yup.'

Bill smiled. 'Been sitting opposite to you

and your quiet colleague for a few hundred miles and you ain't said why you're heading there.'

Clifford glanced at Sam Taylor sitting next to him and shrugged.

'Nope.'

A gunshot sounded outside.

Clifford flexed his hand and pulled his gun. He stared outside into the fog again.

For the barest second the fog parted revealing a line of riders galloping by, their hats set low, their long coats trailing behind them.

'Long coats,' Clifford muttered, jumping to his feet.

'You know what this is about?'

'Got me a few ideas, and it looks like I've struck lucky.'

Clifford pushed back his hat and reached into his pocket for a pair of handcuffs. With a few deft movements, he secured Sam's right hand to his seat and glared at him for a long second. Then he turned to Bill.

'See that you're packing a gun,' Clifford

said. 'You up to using it?'

Bill rubbed his chin. More gunfire sounded from further up the train. 'Suppose so,' Bill said, standing and pulling his gun. 'You some kind of lawman?'

'Nope. I hunt for bounty.'

Clifford turned to the front of the train, stood a moment, and then spun back. With a round-armed punch, he clubbed Sam across the chin, for him to slump over his seat, his eyes closing.

With Clifford taking the lead, the two men dashed down the carriage and through the next two carriages.

The people making this journey were mainly womenfolk and smart-suited city types. Most cowered between the seats.

When Clifford threw open the door to the last carriage, the carriage was empty. He stalked down the aisle, glancing left and right through the windows. Outside, the fog shrouded the carriage, darkening the interior to a murky twilight even in the middle of the afternoon.

Close sporadic gunfire sounded. The dull thud of a body hitting the floor echoed on the other side of the door at the end of the carriage.

Clifford edged to the door. He lifted a hand, halting Bill a few yards back.

'Follow my lead,' Clifford whispered, 'and this'll work out fine.' Bill nodded.

As Clifford reached for the door, it blasted open and a long coated man stood framed in the doorway. Clifford swung round, his gun arcing towards this man. He fired from scant feet away and the man spun back clutching his chest.

Then another man stormed through the doorway, smashing away Clifford's gun with the back of his hand.

Clifford stumbled back between the seats and the man slugged Clifford on the jaw. Clifford collapsed against the window to crash through it in a huge explosion of shattered glass. He landed outside on his shoulder. A dull crack sounded as unconsciousness stole him within seconds.

Back in the carriage, Bill fired, shooting Clifford's attacker through the chest.

As tendrils of fog oozed into the carriage through the broken window, Bill edged forward, his gun held out. He glanced down to check that the man he'd shot was dead.

Another outlaw hurtled through the doorway.

Bill fired at the outlaw, blasting away his gun from his right hand. The outlaw staggered back, shaking his hand. He whistled through pursed lips and grinned.

'That was mighty fine shooting,' he said, his voice level and unconcerned.

Bill nodded. 'Kind of pride myself that I hit what I aim at and I'm aiming at your forehead right now.'

The outlaw nodded and stood sideways to Bill.

'You're right to have pride in that skill, but you've just made two big mistakes.'

'Made a few of those in my life. Two more ain't going to matter.'

'These ones do.'

The outlaw glanced through the broken window and then swung round, his left arm rising with awesome speed.

At the last moment, Bill saw the second gun in the outlaw's left hand and then a bullet ripped into his shoulder. Bill staggered back to collapse between the aisles. He lay a moment and then rolled to his knees.

'You had a second gun,' Bill muttered, clutching his shoulder and wincing at the pain.

With the fog swirling into the carriage and filling in behind him, the outlaw swaggered down the aisle.

'That was your first mistake,' he whispered. 'You obviously didn't know who was raiding this train. If you had, you'd have known I always carry two guns.'

'You're Kirk Morton,' Bill murmured, his bowels turning to ice as he stared into the outlaw's cold eyes.

'Yup. And from your expression, I reckon you've just realized your second mistake.' Kirk slipped his right hand down to his boot and pulled out a long knife. 'Because you've just riled me, and when I'm riled I look for entertainment.'

'Get back,' Bill muttered. He sidled back along the floor until he slammed into the wall.

'No place to hide,' Kirk said and leaned down.

Bill gulped as the knife closed on his face. Framing the knife were Kirk Morton's cold eyes.

2

Nat McBain strode into the jailer's office with Clifford Trantor at his side. As the condemned prisoners' voices echoed in the office, he grabbed Clifford's arm, spinning him around.

'This is a bad idea,' Nat said. 'Let's find another way.'

Clifford shrugged away Nat's hand.

'Yeah, I know your view,' Clifford said, rubbing his shoulder. 'But my shoulder's all mended and I ain't wasting any more time. Either you're with me or you ain't.'

Nat rubbed his forehead and sighed.

'I suppose I'm with you,' Nat snarled. 'But I still don't agree with this.'

Clifford nodded and gestured to the jailer, a tall man with hair turning grey, Rory Johnson.

With a bemused glare, Rory threw open a cupboard beside the door to the condemned prisoners' wing.

Nat and Clifford unhooked their gunbelts and swung them inside the cupboard.

Once Rory had locked the cupboard, he frisked them. Then he rummaged through his collection of keys and unlocked the door.

Beyond the door there was a long corridor with cells along on both sides. An acrid smell hit Nat with an almost solid force. He took a deep breath and followed Rory down the corridor.

Rory maintained a steady pace. He swung his keys and whistled. The sound didn't mask the incessant noise. He alternated turning left and right to sneer in at the cells' occupants.

As he passed each cell, the prisoners jumped off their bunks and dashed to the fronts of their cells. They rattled tin trays against the bars, spat at Rory, and yelled oaths and taunts. Their noise created a wave of solid abuse, drowning out the individual words.

Outside the final cell, Rory stopped and stood to one side.

'This him?' Nat asked, peering into the dank cell.

Rory nodded and glanced through the bars of the door leading from the corridor. A short corridor was beyond, which led to a platform and a noose. Rory sighed.

'You want to speak to him through the bars?'

Nat glanced at Clifford, who shook his head.

'Nope,' Clifford said, 'we'll go in.'

'Your loss,' Rory said with a shrug. 'If he does anything, holler, and I'll get you out. Ain't promising that you'll still be alive, but I'll get you out.'

Clifford smiled. 'I understand, but from what I hear, he ain't that much trouble.'

Rory laughed. With a shake of his head, he rattled open the door. While Clifford strode into the small cell, Nat stood in the entrance and Rory wandered down the corridor.

The prisoner sat on his bunk, the cell's only furniture, with his knees drawn up to his chin, showing none of the ruthlessness that Rory had said he had. He stared at the floor, his eyes so deep-set they were invisible in the poor light. He was haggard, his clothes hanging from his thin frame.

With his arms folded, Clifford waited and eventually the prisoner looked up at him.

'Evening,' Clifford said, 'you'd be Spenser O'Connor.'

The prisoner, Spenser, rubbed his angular bristled chin and grinned at Clifford.

'Might be,' Spenser said, with a slow drawl. 'Depends who wants to see me.'

'The name's Clifford Trantor.' Clifford gestured back. 'And this is Nathaniel McBain.'

Spenser shrugged. 'Ain't one for formal introductions.'

'We guessed that.'

'You ain't lawyers or guards or priests.' Spenser sighed. 'So I'm guessing you're here to ask me what I want for my last meal.'

'I can do that if you want.'

Spenser sneered. 'I ain't ready to order it yet.'

'When will you be ready?'

'Twenty years will be about right.' Spenser widened his eyes, providing a slight gleam in the reflected light. 'Thirty will be better.'

Clifford chuckled. 'Might be offering you that.'

Spenser's grin died and he narrowed his eyes.

'Don't taunt me,' he said, his voice tired beyond his years. 'Go away or I'll show you why I'm in Beaver Ridge jail.'

'Ain't here to taunt you.'

'Then what are you here for?'

'I'm here to talk to you.'

Spenser glanced around his small cell. He released his legs to swing them down to the floor, running them through some rotted strands of straw. With his hands behind his head, he leaned against the cell wall.

'Guess as I ain't doing much,' he said, puffing out his chest, 'so I'm listening.'

Clifford unfolded his arms and walked a short pace to look down at the condemned prisoner.

'From what I hear, you're swinging from a noose at dawn, but if you help me, it don't have to be like that.'

'You offering me a pardon?'

Clifford laughed. 'Dead men don't get pardons.'

'Then what are you offering?'

'A chance of living beyond tomorrow, if you've got the sense to take it.'

'You offering that out of the goodness of

your heart?'

'Nope. You'll live beyond tomorrow if you lead us to someone.' Spenser nodded and spat from the corner of his mouth.

'Should have recognized the type. You're bounty hunters.'

'Yup. We're the best.'

'Then I ain't interested.'

With Spenser lowering his head, Clifford glanced at Nat and nodded. Nat sauntered forward and stood beside Clifford.

'You're lying,' Nat muttered. 'We're offering to get you out of here.'

Spenser looked up, a small smile on his face.

'You're joking. Two bounty hunters can't get me out of a condemned cell.'

'These ones can.'

Spenser chuckled, nodding his head from side to side.

'All right, I'll choose to believe you. Who are you after?'

Nat tipped back his hat and turned. He strode a pace to lean on the bars.

'Kirk Morton,' Nat said.

Spenser laughed, the laughter growing into prolonged guffawing. 'Thanks,' Spenser said, fighting back his laughter while holding his stomach in a parody of extreme mirth. 'Dying men don't get many chances to laugh. I'm thankful for that.'

'This ain't a laughing matter. We're offering you freedom in return for helping us find Kirk Morton.'

Spenser ran his tongue around his lips, suppressing his chuckles. He spat on the floor and shook his head.

'You *are* serious, aren't you?'

'Sure am.'

'Figures. Finding Kirk Morton is about the only thing that could keep a man like me from the noose.'

'So, do we have a deal?'

Spenser grinned and stretched back on his bunk.

From the front of the cell, Nat heard for the first time the insistent dripping of water from the ceiling into the cell.

Spenser ran his tongue around his lips. 'No deal.'

Nat took a deep breath and opened his mouth to argue, but Clifford patted him on the shoulder and he closed his mouth. They backed to the cell door.

Once Nat was outside, Clifford gestured to Rory and waited in the doorway until the jailer returned. Then Clifford sauntered from the cell and leaned on the bars as Rory locked the cell.

When the cell was secure, Clifford glared at Spenser through the bars until he looked up.

'My young friend's offer is genuine and still available, Spenser. Tomorrow you'll be dangling on the end of a short rope. Are you interested in a way out?'

Spenser sighed. 'I'm guessing you ain't come up against Kirk Morton.'

'I have, and that's why I'm dealing with the likes of you, but I've tracked some of the most ornery outlaws over half the states and Kirk ain't the worst of them. He's just the one with the best price.'

'You're wrong,' Spenser said with a shiver despite the oppressive heat. 'Given the choice of death or crossing Kirk, I'll choose death. Any man who gets on the wrong side of him will spend his last days wishing he hadn't.'

'I ain't believing that. Any man would sooner take a chance on life rather than die. Death tomorrow or come with me are your choices. Whatever you say, I'm offering you the better option. It's your choice. What do you say?'

Spenser stood from his bunk and stalked to the front of the cell. He leaned on the bars, stretching, and stared at Clifford, his hooded eyes bright.

'Still no deal.'

Clifford shrugged and turned on his heel. He stared into the cell opposite to Spenser's.

The inmate glanced up and spat on the floor.

'Evening, Sam,' Clifford said.

When Clifford received nothing in return but a glare, he turned to Spenser.

'He a friend of yours?' Spenser said.

Clifford nodded and dawdled from the cell. He had passed the edge of the cell when Spenser coughed.

With a deliberate stamp of his feet, Clifford stopped. He turned and leaned back to look in the cell.

'You trying to get my attention?'

Spenser stared at the floor and spat down.

'You say that you're taking in Kirk for the bounty?'

'Yup. He's coming in dead or alive.'

Spenser nodded. 'And if I help, I avoid the noose and leave here permanently?'

'That was the deal.'

'Perhaps I was hasty,' Spenser said with a long sigh.

'Perhaps you were, but you ain't listening.' Clifford grinned. 'That *was* the deal. You turned it down and so I'm leaving. But I'll ask the guards to find out what you want for your last meal.'

'You what?' Spenser roared, slamming his fist against the bars.

Clifford ignored him and strode down the corridor after Nat and Rory, braving the tunnel of abuse and spit. From behind, Spenser's oaths merged into the other prisoners' torrent of curses.

Once they'd closed the door to the condemned cells, Nat turned to Clifford and shrugged.

'Got to ask you,' Nat said. 'Why turn him down? He was ready to help us.'

'True, but he ain't as motivated as I want him to be.'

Nat batted dregs of spit from his clothes.

'If you want to go back in there to get him more motivated, you're doing it on your own.'

Clifford shrugged. 'Don't panic. We'll let him sleep on it. In the morning he'll have reached the right level of motivation.'

Clifford wandered into Jed's saloon, situated on the outskirts of Beaver Ridge, and nodded at his fairhaired partner.

'Where we're going,' Clifford said, 'we won't get many chances to relax. Reckon as we ought to enjoy ourselves for a while.'

Nat grinned. 'I like that kind of thought.'

For an hour they leaned on the bar and knocked back a few whiskeys, washing away the trail dust.

'So where are we heading?' Nat asked.

'Last I heard, Kirk was in the hills to the north of Prudence.'

Nat took a long sip of his whiskey.

'You ain't told me and I ain't asked, but if you're hell bent on taking Spenser with us, I ought to know. What has Spenser done to deserve the noose?'

'Unsure of all his crimes, but he rode with Kirk Morton before he struck out on his own, so that's more than enough to swing. A few weeks ago, he killed a man in a poker game and ended up in Beaver Ridge jail.'

'Even if Spenser helps us find Kirk, we're doing nobody any favours if Spenser walks free afterwards.'

Clifford shrugged and leaned over his whiskey, sighing under his breath.

'I told you,' Nat whispered when Clifford stayed quiet, 'I ain't happy with you keeping secrets from me.'

'So you want to know everything do you?'

'Yup.'

'That mean you're backing out if you don't like what you hear?'

Nat knocked back his whiskey. He contemplated his empty glass and then refilled it.

In truth, he was unsure what his intentions were.

For the last two years he'd worked as a deputy to his friend Sheriff Cassidy Yates. He owed Cassidy a lot. Nat's pa had lived on the wrong side of the law and that life had tempted the young Nat. But Cassidy had seen the potential in him and persuaded him to try the lawman life. Recently though, Nat had wondered if there might be a better life for him than being a deputy lawman.

He enjoyed the itinerant life and the

excitement that came as routine, but he hated the pay that gave no appreciation of the risks that he took every day. He'd often looked at the posters of wanted outlaws, the bounty more than he'd earn in a year.

Two months ago, Cassidy had left on a mission that he didn't need him for. And so Nat had sat alone in the sheriff's office in Beaver Ridge when Clifford Trantor had arrived searching for the latest information about the outlaw, Kirk Morton.

Kirk had been at large for five years terrorizing remote frontier towns with his gang of outlaws, although his specific crimes were unclear as the authorities laid practically every unsolved crime at his feet.

What was certain was the sadistic nature of Kirk's raids and that recently his gang had attacked several trains. This latter crime, rather than the others, had resulted in the rail companies posting a substantial price on his head.

At the time, Nat had provided Clifford with the information he had, which was less than what Clifford already knew, and returned to sitting leaning back in his chair.

But later that day, Nat had ripped Kirk's poster from the wall. With his head in his hands, he'd stared at the number five followed by three zeros above Kirk's face and the thought had pounded in his mind that being a lawman might not be his only option in life.

That night he'd sought out Clifford and they'd formed a partnership, agreeing to take equal pickings from Kirk's bounty, a decision Nat already thought he'd live to regret.

Nat sighed. 'I ain't backing out.'

'Glad to hear it, Nathaniel.'

'Stick to calling me Nat. I answered to Nathaniel when I was a lawman. Those days are behind me.'

'Nat it is.'

Nat sighed. 'Still got to ask you. Are you keeping your word and letting Spenser go free or are you returning him to jail when we get Kirk?'

Clifford drew in his breath through his teeth and glanced to the side. He nodded towards a man, who sauntered across the saloon to them, his hat pulled low over one side of his face.

'I ain't answering,' Clifford said, 'but you can ask this man if you want.'

The newcomer nodded to Clifford and glanced at Nat. Then he grabbed a spare glass, filling it brimful of whiskey.

As the newcomer leaned over the bar, he exposed a patchwork of scars across the left-hand side of his face, beneath the hat brim.

'Evening, Bill,' Clifford said.

The scarred man, Bill, nodded to them and knocked back half of his whiskey.

'Been waiting for you,' Bill said, his voice gruff. 'I'm ready to move on out when you are.'

Clifford nodded. 'We go first thing in the morning, so you got time for a few more whiskeys.'

'I like the sound of that.' Bill knocked back the remainder of his whiskey and poured another. 'You got Spenser O'Connor with you?'

'Picking him up in the morning.'

With Bill turning to lean over his whiskey, Nat patted Clifford on the arm and beckoned him along the bar.

'You never said,' he whispered, 'that we were getting more company.'

Clifford shrugged. 'You never asked about more company.'

'Don't mock me,' Nat muttered. 'I only just agreed to your damn fool plan to get Spenser O'Connor out of Beaver Ridge's jail, but I ain't happy about more people joining us.'

'There ain't. Bill is the only one.'

From down the bar, Bill glanced at them. He pushed his whiskey from him and sauntered a few paces to join them.

'I'm guessing your young friend ain't happy about me joining you,' Bill said. 'If that's so he'll pay me the courtesy of saying that to my face.'

Nat rolled his shoulders and stood straight.

'I ain't happy about you joining us.'

Bill cracked the knuckles of his right hand. 'Why?'

'I made a deal with Clifford about the bounty and I stick by my word. Ain't many people in this line of work that'll do that, but I intend to, and I believed Clifford was that kind of man too. Seems I was wrong.'

Bill shrugged. 'Your deal still stands.'

Nat sipped his whiskey. 'Then where do you fit in?'

'I'm coming along to help.'

'Nobody comes along to help face someone like Kirk Morton.'

Bill leaned his head to one side and pushed his hat up, letting Nat see the full extent of his ruined features.

Nat gulped.

Bill pulled down his hat. 'Do you want to guess who did that to me?'

Nat lowered his head a moment and took a long sip of his whiskey.

'Nope. When did you meet Kirk?'

'Two months ago, he raided a train and he

was looking for fun. I was part of the fun, but I was lucky. Some others weren't so lucky, so it's up to me to track him down.'

'And you're telling me that you ain't interested in the bounty?'

'Nope. The requirement is to bring in Kirk either dead or alive. Clifford's promised me that we'll try to take him alive. But he'll be dead when we hand him in. I'll ensure his features are intact so there's no problem with the bounty, but the rest of him won't be so lucky.'

Nat stared down at his whiskey.

'I ain't taking chances to capture Kirk alive.'

'And neither am I. If you want to keep those pretty features of yours intact, don't take chances yourself.'

Nat gulped down the rest of his whiskey. He shook the empty bottle and then ordered another bottle.

'And does your deal with Clifford on Kirk Morton's fate go for Spenser O'Connor too?'

Bill grinned. 'Yup.'

Nat leaned over the bar. He rubbed his chin and then pulled the cork of the second bottle of whiskey.

3

As the first rays of morning light filtered across Beaver Ridge's jail, Nat and Clifford sauntered around the outside of the condemned wing. To avoid running the gauntlet of prisoners again, they entered the wing from the other side.

Once inside they stood to the side of the door into the condemned cells. Down the corridor there was a small quadrangle containing a platform on which the guards would hang Spenser. From the gantry a noose swayed in the morning breeze.

They waited until a row of jailers led today's condemned prisoner along his last walk.

Rory headed the jailers. When he saw Nat and Clifford, he nodded and they backed to the wall to ensure Spenser wouldn't see them until the last possible moment.

Spenser shuffled through the door, his head hung, his gait slow. Clifford took a long pace forward.

'Morning, Spenser,' he said. 'Sleep well?'

'You,' Spenser said, glancing up from the floor, his voice high-pitched and his eyes wide with relief. He coughed and nodded. 'Reckoned as you wouldn't give up.'

Clifford ran his gaze up and down the prisoner, lingering on the handcuffs and chains.

'And I reckoned you needed another night to think about your choices.' He glanced down the corridor at the platform. 'So what's it to be?'

Spenser set his feet as wide as his short chains allowed.

'You got my attention. What's the deal?'

Clifford leaned against the corridor wall.

'It's simple. You either walk down this

corridor to the noose or you walk in the other direction with us.'

Spenser nodded over Clifford's shoulder. 'And what's in the other direction?'

'A horse, which you'll mount and help us find Kirk Morton.'

Spenser licked his lips. 'What's the other parts of this offer?'

Clifford took a deep breath. 'You can guess the gist but so there's no misunderstandings – you get no gun, no leeway and no second chances. If you try to escape, I'll kill you. If I think for one second that you're playing games, I'll kill you. If you try anything that I ain't sanctioned, I'll kill you. If you–'

'I get the idea, but I ain't interested in that. What happens after you've got Kirk?'

'Once I've collected on him, you get a chance to run.'

Spenser narrowed his eyes. 'No pardon?'

'Like I told you.' Clifford leaned forward, grinning. 'Dead men don't get pardons.'

'So you're asking me to trust that a bounty hunter will let me go?' Spenser rattled his chains. 'What assurances do I get?'

'Your only assurance is that noose at the end of the corridor if you don't take my offer. Got a problem with that?'

Spenser glanced over his shoulder at the platform. 'Yeah. I need an assurance.'

Clifford sighed. 'Not possible, but I'll tell you this – you're a waste of skin, but Kirk Morton is worth his weight in gold. After I have him, I don't care what you do with your worthless life. If you've got sense you'll crawl into the nearest hole and hide out for life. If you do that, nobody will care about your crimes and you can live a long life.'

Spenser sighed and glanced down at his chains.

'Guessing as I know where I'm heading.'

Clifford grinned. 'I thought you would.'

Once they were outside the condemned wing, Spenser stood beside Clifford's spare horse with his hands out.

Rory Johnson rummaged through his keys and selected the key to Spenser's chains. He stared at it and hunched his shoulders.

From the corner of his eye, he glanced at Clifford.

With a deep intake of breath, Clifford snarled and grabbed Rory's shoulder. He dragged him from their horses to stand beside the jail wall. Clifford glanced back to confirm they were out of earshot of Nat and Spenser. Then he glared at Rory.

'What's the problem?' Clifford muttered.

Rory sighed. 'You know what the problem is. I'm letting a condemned prisoner go free. I ain't paid to do that.'

'Yeah, but you agreed to take on the problems. The sooner we're gone, the sooner you can sort them.'

Rory wiped his hand across his forehead to swipe away a layer of sweat.

'I've been sorting them for the last week and I'll be sorting them for the rest of my life, which will be short if certain people work out what I've done.'

Clifford rubbed his chin.

'You'd better not be aiming for a bigger payment, because I've paid you everything you'll get.' Clifford lowered his hat and kicked at a stone. 'If you're having second thoughts, you've picked the wrong man to make your enemy.'

'No second thoughts, but I have reconsidered. Expenses to organize this were a lot higher than I expected. I had to–'

'I don't care what you had to do,' Clifford snapped. He glanced at the waiting Spenser and Nat and lowered his voice. 'Look. We had a deal and you can't back out. I have nothing more to give you. You cleaned me out to set this up.'

Rory shrugged. 'Ain't asking for more today.'

'Then what are you asking for?'

'I want a cut of the bounty too, when you've collected it.'

Clifford took a deep breath. 'I can see you've reckoned that you have me where you want me, but I'm the wrong man to try this on. I've put enough money into this. If other jackals are looking for a cut, it ain't worth my while to get Kirk and I walk away.'

'Yeah, but the rail companies have just decided that a raid from a few months ago was Kirk's work and they've increased his price to six thousand dollars.'

'Didn't take me that long to decide it was him,' Clifford muttered, rubbing his shoulder. He whistled through his teeth and nodded. 'Perhaps in the circumstances I can be more generous. You get another three hundred when I have Kirk. Will that help those keys to loosen?'

Rory nodded and gestured with Spenser's chain key.

'You know, it might at that.'

Clifford followed Rory to the waiting prisoner, tempering his irritation at not offering Rory less – as clearly Rory was expecting a lower offer, with the thought of the bounty having risen.

Once Rory had released Spenser's chains, Spenser rubbed his wrists and stretched with extravagant gestures.

Rory wandered to the condemned wing, shaking his head.

With his hands on his hips, Clifford watched Rory go and then turned to Spenser.

'Do I need to go through the rules that'll keep you alive again?' Clifford asked.

'Nope,' Spenser said, shaking his head and glancing around. 'I know where I stand.'

In a slow gesture, Clifford held out his hands before him and nodded at Spenser's hands.

'Hey,' Spenser whined. 'I just got out of chains.'

Clifford shrugged and unhooked a length of rope from his horse.

'And you'll get out of this,' Clifford muttered, tying the rope tight around Spenser's wrists. 'But only if you earn the privilege.'

Without further word, Clifford mounted his horse and after a couple of ungainly jumps, Spenser rolled into his saddle. Once Nat had mounted, they trotted through the opened gates of Beaver Ridge jail.

Nat and Clifford gazed ahead, wondering

whether to believe Rory's promises that they could leave with Spenser.

Spenser glanced around too, a wide grin on his face. He nodded at the guards as they passed through the gates. Once they were fifty yards from the gates, he produced a prolonged yell of delight and released the reins to slap his thigh with his hat.

'I got to hand it to you,' he shouted. 'You got me this far. It was worth it to breathe free air again.'

'Glad you think so,' Clifford said, pulling his horse to a halt and standing across the trail. 'Because that's the last time you're making a noise I ain't authorized.'

Spenser nodded and glanced away, still grinning.

Clifford hunched his shoulders and turned to the trail.

From out of the undergrowth Bill rode, hunched forward in the saddle. His scars wrinkled when he saw Spenser.

'Who're you?' Spenser muttered.

Bill chuckled. 'I'm their new partner.'

'Why you staring at me?'

'You know,' Bill said and held his head to one side.

Spenser gulped. 'Guessing as that's Kirk's handiwork.'

'Yup, but I remember that he had help and one of those helpers was you.'

Spenser shrugged. 'I don't remember you.'

'You probably can't remember everyone you've hurt.' Bill grinned and lowered his voice. 'I've got the better memory and I sure can remember you.'

Clifford gripped the reins and turned from Bill.

'Come on,' Clifford said with a sigh. 'Ain't got time for pleasant chat. We got some travelling ahead of us.'

For most of the fine spring morning the group rode at a steady pace without conversation. Spenser rode ahead of Clifford and Bill, with Nat at the rear. At all times Clifford glared at Spenser's back.

When the trail widened, Nat drew his

horse in beside Clifford.

'If'n you can't keep your gaze off Spenser,' Nat said, 'he ain't the sort of man who should be loose.'

Clifford shook his head. 'He's the perfect man to be loose. For a start he's someone a former lawman like you don't recognize.'

'What you mean?'

'If I picked a man who wasn't a minor outlaw like Spenser O'Connor, someone would recognize him and might take exception to him being free.'

'You may be right, but I want to know if you have more surprises.'

Clifford kept his gaze on the trail and Spenser.

'What's that supposed to mean?'

'Such as the bribes you agreed with that jailer, Rory Johnson.'

'That was a surprise?'

Nat sighed and ran a hand over his forehead.

'Nope. What did it cost to get out this minor outlaw?'

‘Six hundred dollars after that last piece of negotiation. You got a problem with that?’

‘Nope, but I wonder why you thought you had to hide it from me.’

Clifford sighed, staring straight ahead.

‘I didn’t know what a former lawman might think of that.’

‘This former lawman knows that your sort needs bribes to capture the likes of Kirk Morton, but any man hates discovering his partner is hiding something. So forget I used to be a lawman. If you’re planning on doing something you think I’ll hate, tell me about it and we’ll discuss what to do, but I’m telling you, I hate secrets.’

Clifford took a deep breath. ‘Understood.’

‘So you reckon we have everything we need now?’

‘Yup. Any more men and the bounty split wouldn’t make it worthwhile. Any less men and we’d end up dead.’

‘Reckon as there’s a good chance of that anyhow. Three men and Spenser O’Connor don’t seem much to face Kirk Morton and his gang.'

'It will be. I'd have had him a few months back if one of his men hadn't got a lucky drop on me and knocked me unconscious.'

'So you claim, but you had no choice about facing him then. You do now.'

'I've put too much time and money into this.' Clifford shrugged. 'The choices I gave Spenser were death or bounty and those are our choices too.'

Nat sighed and hunched over his horse.

4

When the group had travelled for three days they approached Prudence, the next major town on the western trail.

Nat had expected Spenser to try to escape, but he was the ideal travelling partner, saying little and joining in the chores needed for a long journey. Even so, Clifford never took his gaze from Spenser. Even when Clifford was asleep, he seemed to know exactly where Spenser was and what he was doing.

After Prudence, the group of riders headed north into the hills. With each mile, the trail became less defined and the ground rockier as they entered the less travelled parts of Kansas.

Around noon, Spenser slowed his horse to ride alongside Clifford. 'So,' he said, 'as you ain't asked me where to go yet, I reckon you know where you're heading.'

'Yup.'

'So you'll only need me when we're closer to Kirk?'

'Yup.'

Spenser sighed. 'And when we get where you're heading, you reckon a travelling man like Kirk will be there?'

'Nope.'

'So if you ain't asking me, what's your great method of finding Kirk?'

'I have simple methods.'

Spenser licked his lips. 'Amuse me.'

Clifford turned to Spenser and smiled.

'I walk into a saloon and ask for information.'

Spenser raised his eyebrows. 'That subtle.'

'I stick with what works.'

'If I'm to be part of this group, I reckon I have a better way of getting information on Kirk's latest whereabouts.'

'You ain't here to have better ideas, just to help when we're closer to Kirk.'

'Carry on,' Spenser said, lifting his bound hands high and speeding his horse. 'I'm enjoying my freedom.'

Nobody said anything more until early afternoon when they reached a trading post at the joining of the north trail to another west trail. Outside the trading post, Clifford dismounted and nodded to Bill.

'You look after him while we've gone,' Clifford said.

Bill grinned and turned to Spenser.

'Keep those ideas of yours quiet, Spenser,' Bill muttered. 'I ain't convinced you got a right to carry on living.'

Nat jumped down from his horse and followed Clifford into the trading post.

Inside there was the usual collection of drifters, drinkers and rough types drinking away the afternoon.

Clifford glanced around. As he didn't recognize anyone, he sauntered to the bar – three planks of wood set over upturned barrels.

Nat edged past the large piles of provisions that filled half of the room and joined Clifford.

'Clifford,' Nat said, 'why not listen to what Spenser has to say if he has information?'

'Because I'm stopping him getting uppity until I have no choice.'

'But we bought him out of jail to use him.'

'I know. But we need to keep him under control until we get closer to Kirk. Then his knowledge of Kirk's tactics will be invaluable.'

Clifford grabbed an empty glass and banged it on the bar with an insistent tap until the trading-post folk's conversation drifted to silence.

'Right,' he shouted, his voice echoing through the room. 'The name's Clifford Trantor and I'm a man with money available for information.'

Moving his hand slow, Clifford reached into his pocket and pulled out a wad of notes. He waved these over his head and then slipped them into his pocket.

'What kind of information you looking for?' a bearded man asked, looking up from his drink.

'The accurate kind.' Clifford leaned his face down to inches from the bearded man and smiled. 'The kind that gives me no reason to return and reclaim my money.'

The bearded man chuckled. 'On any particular subject?'

'I'm a bounty hunter.' Clifford smiled as several people examined their drinks with excessive interest. 'I'm looking for a man who passed through here two months ago. Guessing as some of you were here when he did, and I'm also guessing someone knows where he was heading and what his plans were.'

'You talking about Kirk Morton?'

Clifford nodded. 'I reckoned you were someone with plenty of information.'

'You might be right at that, but you're behind everyone looking for Kirk Morton. If I charged everyone looking for Kirk a dollar for information on where he'd gone,' the bearded man patted his fingers together, mouthing numbers, 'let's say I'd have enough for a few whiskeys.'

Clifford placed the glass on the bar.

'Who else is looking for him?'

The bearded man shrugged. 'Other bounty hunters, all kinds of lawmen. Most people want to know where Kirk headed so they can go the other way.'

'Figures. What do you tell them?'

'I tell them he went west,' the bearded man said with a smile.

'Information like that won't buy many whiskeys.'

'Only information I got. I could invent something to earn more, but I don't like dealing with your sort. I trust Kirk more than I trust you.'

Several trading-post folk chuckled, but Clifford had seen one man who was ignoring this exchange. The man sat behind a table, his hat low, staring at his hands in his lap.

Clifford turned from the bearded man and sauntered across the room.

'You look like the kind of fellow who knows more information than this man.'

With extreme slowness, the man looked up. He tipped back his hat to reveal deep-blue eyes framed in a mass of dirt. With a gloved hand, he rubbed his grimed forehead.

'Why do you think that?' he murmured.

'I just reckon you do.'

Still moving slowly, the man stood from the table and drew to his full height. He grinned when he found he had a few inches on Clifford.

'You shouldn't bother asking more questions.'

'Perhaps you're right.' Clifford rolled his shoulders. 'You ain't bright enough to answer.'

The man snorted. He glanced away and then swirled round to punch Clifford in the guts.

As Clifford had anticipated the blow, he rolled with the punch and swung his elbow round to smash his forearm across the attacker's face.

With a cry, the man fell back. But two more men leapt to their feet from nearby tables and charged Clifford.

With a whirl of his fist, Clifford clubbed the first attacker on the chin, but the second man reached him a moment later and bundled him to the table. As Clifford fell, he grabbed the man's jacket and pulled him back too. When he rolled over the table and hit the floor, Clifford kicked back to throw his assailant over his shoulder.

Clifford lay winded a moment and then

rolled to his feet. He glanced to the bar, searching for Nat, but Nat was squaring off to another man. Clifford clubbed down another attacker and dashed to Nat as Nat hurled his assailant over the bar.

Nat turned, his eyes wide.

'Watch out,' he yelled.

Clifford ducked, the action saving him from a club, which whistled over his head. He turned.

A grinning man held a broken chair-leg in an outstretched hand, three other men flanking him.

The grinning man laughed. 'You chose the wrong time and place to ask questions.'

Clifford shrugged and with a round-footed kick, bundled the grinning man to the floor. As the man fell, Clifford wrenched the club from his hand and swung it up and around, knocking the second man on the jaw. The fellow stood straight and collapsed to the floor.

Nat bundled the third man to the floor with a flurry of blows to the stomach and with an almost casual gesture, Clifford swung the club round, hitting this man across the back of the head. The club resounded with a dull thud.

Clifford rolled his shoulders and swung back the club ready to hit the last man, but Nat floored this man with a solid blow to the chin. With their assailants down, Clifford leaned against the bar. He flexed his fists and smiled at the remaining trading post folk who weren't flat out on the floor.

'Now that we've got that sorted,' he said, shrugging his jacket closed, 'anybody else withholding information?'

The remaining people made a big show of not looking at him. Clifford glared at the bearded man.

'Seems that you have the best information in here. So what is it?' Clifford patted his club.

'West is all I know,' the bearded man said, shaking.

Clifford tapped the club against the bar. 'West ain't enough.'

The bearded man stared at the club and shook his head. 'West is all I got.'

With an angry shrug, Clifford glared around the trading post.

At his feet, one of their attackers was grumbling as he came conscious.

Clifford tapped a foot against the man's side, receiving a groan. 'Any of these men know anything.'

The bearded man shook his head. 'We know nothing.'

'Except west,' Clifford muttered and threw the club on the prone man's chest.

He stalked outside, Nat following a few paces back, and sauntered to his horse.

'So,' Spenser said, looking up and grinning, 'where we heading?'

'West,' Clifford muttered.

Spenser glanced down at Clifford's battered clothes.

'Looks like you went to an awful lot of trouble to get that one word.'

'I didn't ask you for a view.'

While Clifford and Nat batted down their

clothes, Bill sighed.

'Thought that's all you'd get,' Bill said. 'Kirk often passes through here with good reason. Guess he's still got friends around these parts.'

Clifford rubbed his chin. 'Yeah. Perhaps when we're further west, I'll take Spenser up on his offer and let him do the questioning. He needs that cockiness beaten out of him.'

Spenser nodded with a wide grin. 'I did offer. You got to start trusting me. If I'd done the questioning I'd have received better answers than the one word you got.'

Clifford batted the last of the dust from his clothes and sighed.

'So what would you have done?'

Spenser rolled his tongue around his lips and stared at the trading post.

'I'd have picked the right people to ask, and I'd have asked questions those right people might answer. Except, as you don't trust me, I ain't putting myself out.'

With a quick kick, Clifford knocked away

a stone at his feet. 'You will if I say you will.'

'Your threats mean nothing. If you don't like anything I say, you can kill me, but then you don't get Kirk.'

Clifford shrugged and mounted his horse. As Nat mounted his own horse, Clifford swung his steed towards the western trail. He lifted the reins high. Then with a sigh, he lowered them and turned to Spenser.

'All right, let's hear what you've been thinking.'

Spenser tipped back his hat and glanced at the trading post.

'I been thinking that you've been in a fight and before long somebody will come out of that trading post. When they do, they won't use their fists.'

'Then you'll be on the receiving end too unless you know how to defend yourself, but we're staying here until you tell me what you've been thinking.'

Spenser sighed. 'I been thinking that I ain't enthused enough with finding Kirk to bother asking the questions you need answers to.'

With a steady glance from Bill to Nat, Clifford nodded. 'Talk like that can get a man killed.'

'Talk like that is all you're getting from someone who ain't enthused.'

Clifford whistled through his teeth. 'Go on. What would enthuse you?'

'I overheard that jailer in Beaver Ridge jail. I hadn't realized how valuable Kirk Morton is. Six thousand dollars is an awful lot of money for one man.'

'It is. Otherwise I wouldn't be on his tail.'

Spenser licked his lips. 'With all that money, ten per cent is a fair price for a member of the team that brings him in.'

Clifford chuckled. 'Glad to see you have a sense of humour. All you're getting out of this is avoiding that noose.'

'You saw a few of Kirk's casual friends in there and got some bruises. They're the least ornery of his friends you'll be meeting. Most wouldn't waste two seconds' thought before killing you and the rest are worse.

Any man who crosses Kirk will have plenty of people set against him and avoiding the noose ain't enough. I need money to get far away. And ten per cent of six thousand dollars will do that.'

A long whistle came from Clifford's lips as he gripped the reins tight.

'For ten per cent I'll need your full co-operation.'

'You what?' Nat shouted but Clifford raised a hand silencing him.

Spenser smiled. 'For ten per cent you'll get it.'

'So, Mr Ten Per Cent, where do you suggest we go?'

With his bound hands, Spenser pointed south.

'Back to Prudence.'

As Clifford turned his horse south, Nat shook his head.

'Clifford,' he muttered, 'we need to talk.'

'Later, Nat,' Clifford said and winked at Nat.

'Now,' Nat shouted, but Clifford shook his

reins and with Bill and Spenser headed down the trail.

Nat gritted his teeth and watched them leave. But seeing no choice, he took a deep breath and followed.

5

A few hours after sunset the group arrived in Prudence. The town was building up the traditional night bustle, with music blasting from most saloons and excited people milling about.

'Time you decided whether you trust me,' Spenser muttered as they pulled up outside the saloon he'd indicated.

Clifford dismounted and strolled round to stand beside Spenser's horse.

'Done that, and I don't.'

Spenser chuckled. 'Fine, but your methods failed to get information. And so will mine with my hands tied.'

Clifford took long deep breaths. Then he reached down to his boot and, with a great swipe of his knife, severed Spenser's bonds.

'So what's your great plan?'

Spenser rubbed his wrists and glanced at the saloon.

'I'll direct questions to the sort of people who'd never give an answer to the likes of you.'

'Seems reasonable,' Clifford said, waving his arm to the saloon. 'Ask away.'

Spenser scratched his chin and smiled.

'I'll need your help.' Spenser rubbed his fingers together.

'Is that the kind of help I reckon you mean?' Clifford said, narrowing his eyes.

'Yeah.'

Clifford gritted his teeth. 'How much?'

'Fifty dollars should be about right.'

'Fifty dollars,' Clifford shouted. 'You can buy an awful lot of information for fifty dollars. Find someone cheaper or I'll run out of funds before I get within a hundred miles of Kirk Morton.'

'I ain't buying information and I ain't losing your money.'

With his eyes still narrowed, Clifford glared up at Spenser.

'What's that mean?'

'It means I'm playing poker.'

Clifford sighed. 'In that case I'm coming with you.'

He ordered Bill and Nat to camp down outside town and then followed Spenser into the saloon.

Inside, Spenser sauntered across the room and leaned on the bar. He surveyed the saloon folk and the numerous groups chatting amongst themselves. Three poker games were in progress by the back wall.

Clifford leaned on the bar beside Spenser.

'Which game we joining?' Clifford asked.

Spenser grinned. 'None of these and keep quiet.'

As Clifford glared at him, Spenser turned and gestured to the bartender for a whiskey. When the bartender sauntered to him,

Spenser leaned over the bar and whispered something to him.

The bartender shrugged. He served them two whiskeys and sauntered back along the bar.

'What happens now?' Clifford asked.

'You get patience. That's what happens now.'

They supped their whiskeys in silence for twenty minutes. Then a man dressed in smarter clothes than anyone else in the saloon filtered from the crowd and tapped Spenser on the back.

Spenser nodded and beckoned Clifford with a finger.

'Only you,' the smart man said, glaring at Clifford.

'He's all right,' Spenser said. 'I can vouch for him.'

The smart man shrugged and turned. He led them up the side stairs and down a first floor corridor which snaked left and right. Squealing and giggling emerged from the rooms along the corridor. At the end of this corridor, he threw open a door.

With a short nod, Clifford peered in, wondering what he'd see. Inside the room, five men sat around a table filled with half-empty whiskey bottles, playing quiet, concentrated poker. The men were smoking a variety of cigars and cheroots and the room was thick with their stench, a blue haze swirling in the light from the ring of oil-lamps on the sideboards.

Clifford hated smokes and fought to suppress a cough.

They waited beside the door until the current hand ended.

With a few silent nods, the men shuffled round to provide space for Clifford and Spenser, but making them sit apart.

For three hours they played pure poker. The other players weren't big city gamblers with high stakes and nerves to match, and the pot never rose above ten dollars, but each man played as if his life depended on the current hand.

Clifford wasn't an expert and he lost at a

steady rate, although Spenser steadily added to his funds.

Clifford's shoulders relaxed as he accepted that Spenser wouldn't try to escape, and he began to enjoy being surrounded with what he took for the dregs of the town.

When a one-hundred-dollar pot arrived for the first time, a straight battle broke out between two men, and when the bets were down and they revealed hands – four eights against a full house – a round of appreciating chuckles drifted around the table.

Clifford tensed, expecting trouble, but instead the loser smiled and pushed from the table.

'This ain't my night,' he said. 'I'm down to my last few cents.'

The winner smiled and threw back a few dollars from his winnings.

'If you're leaving, I'll stake you some fun.'

Everyone chuckled as the loser tipped his hat and sauntered from the room, calling to the saloon's Madame.

With this break, everyone stood from the

table and stretched. Clifford stood beside the door and listened to Spenser talk with a portly man, whom he learned was Jim Stark.

'Surprised to see you, Spenser,' Jim said.

Spenser shrugged. 'I enjoy a game of poker as much as the next man.'

'Didn't mean that.' Jim rubbed a hand over his jowls. 'From what I heard, you're dead.'

Spenser laughed. 'Takes more than a few scrapes to kill me.'

'Maybe, but I also heard you got yourself arrested and hung.'

'You heard wrong.' Spenser wrapped his hands around his neck and waggled his head from side to side with his mouth wide open. 'If I was all strung up, I wouldn't be here.'

'Yeah, but I'm guessing that you ain't heading to Beaver Ridge.'

'That's true.' Spenser leaned close and placed his hand beside his mouth, lowering his voice so that Clifford could just hear him. 'Had a spot of trouble there. I barely got away. If I hadn't, what you heard happened to me would have happened.'

'Understood. What you doing now?'

Spenser sighed and stared at the poker table. 'I'm heading north. Might join some old friends.'

Jim nodded. 'Guessing you mean Kirk Morton?'

Spenser glanced around. Only Clifford was close.

'I ain't saying that.'

'Yeah, but I ain't heard about Kirk for a while.'

'I heard different. Anyhow, what you doing these days?'

As Jim told him about his recent exploits, Clifford gritted his teeth and tried to catch Spenser's eye to encourage him to press for more details, but Spenser chatted about irrelevant matters until the game restarted.

In irritation at Spenser's lack of questioning, Clifford didn't concentrate on the next two hands, and when his breathing calmed, he was down to his last three dollars.

The man sitting beside him glanced at Clifford's few notes.

'Hoping you got plenty more where that came from,' he said, grinning.

Clifford was about to boast, but then shrugged.

'Nope. My luck needs to change.'

Everybody laughed and leaned over the table for the next hand. Clifford lost again and pushed from the table.

'Looks like my luck's deserted me tonight. I'll just watch.'

Jim shook his head. 'You either play or go, but we ain't having spectators.'

Each card-player glared up at Clifford, hands drifting below the table or near their gunbelts.'

'I ain't trouble.'

'Good. Then you'll be leaving.'

Clifford glared at Spenser, who shuffled the deck and stared at the table.

Clifford sighed. 'Looks like we're leaving, Spenser.'

Spenser glanced up and shrugged. 'Looks like *you* are leaving. My luck is better than yours is. I'll stay until I've cleaned everyone out.'

Choice comments greeted this boast.

Clifford leaned on the table, thrusting his face a few inches from Spenser's.

'You didn't hear me,' he said, enunciating each word. 'We are leaving.'

Jim stood. 'Hey, what you threatening him for?'

'I ain't.' Clifford glanced around the circle of men. 'I staked him tonight's fun. As he's playing with my money, I get to say whether he stays or goes.'

A ring of guns lifted and pointed at Clifford's and Spenser's heads.

With his hands flat on the table, Clifford could only stare at each man in turn.

'Now,' he whispered, 'why have you gone and done that?'

'Stop!' Spenser shouted, lifting his hands high. 'Clifford didn't mean that. We ain't working together. He meant that I owed him money and if I'd repaid him, I couldn't get a stake in this game.'

Jim holstered his gun. 'All right, I believe Spenser ain't a cheat. Besides, if he was he'd have won more than he has.'

The man opposite to Jim shrugged. 'Agreed, but Spenser is leaving. I don't trust him now.'

Spenser stood. 'Yeah. I understand.'

With a last glance at Clifford, Spenser sauntered to the door.

Clifford glanced at the poker players, but they were already hunched over the next hand.

With a shrug, he followed Spenser. He stalked a few paces back as Spenser wandered along the winding corridor, down the stairs, through the saloon and outside. Once they were outside, he slammed a hand on Spenser's shoulder and pulled him round.

'You heard my warning in Beaver Ridge jail but you ignored it. You get no choices, no options, or no opportunity to double-cross on our deal. Only thing keeping you alive is I don't know what you tried back there.'

Spenser shrugged. 'I wasn't trying anything but getting us information.'

Clifford shook his head and dragged Spenser down the road.

Spenser kicked his heels, but Clifford gripped tighter. Then Spenser relaxed and let Clifford throw him to his horse.

Once they reached the campsite Clifford dismounted. He hauled Spenser from his horse and threw him towards the camp-fire.

'Your life's on a knife-edge, Spenser,' Clifford muttered. 'You ain't taking me for a fool. Sit and keep quiet.'

Spenser glared and then sat, hunching up his knees to his chin.

'What's wrong?' Nat asked.

Clifford unhooked the rope from his horse and stalked to Spenser. 'Spenser wasn't trying to get information from our poker game. It was a ploy to try and escape.'

'It wasn't,' Spenser whined.

'Only failed because I dragged you out of

that game.' Clifford turned to Nat. 'I reckon he had a plan. The poker game was for men who had a stake. As soon as you'd lost your stake you had to leave. He figured I'd lose first. Then he'd escape.'

Spenser rummaged in his pocket and pulled out a wad of notes.

'If that was my plan,' Spenser said, 'it would have worked. You're terrible at poker.'

Nat chuckled. 'You lost your fifty dollars, Clifford?'

'Yeah,' Clifford muttered.

'Can see why you're in a bad mood.'

Spenser riffled through his notes. He peeled off a handful and held them out to Clifford.

'As we're a team, you should get back your one hundred dollars.'

'I ain't taking money from you.' Clifford sighed. With an angry lunge he snatched the notes. He glared at the rope in his other hand and then threw it towards his horse. 'That's your last warning. I'm leaving you untied because I'm encouraging you to try something else. When you do, it'll be your last act.'

Spenser shook his head. 'That was no trick.'

'Ain't believing that. We were in there for hours and you didn't ask about Kirk Morton. The only person you spoke to knew squat.'

Spenser shrugged. 'So we're using your methods from now on, are we?'

'If I start thinking like that, I got no use for you.' Clifford grinned, leaving the threat unvoiced.

'Then I'm glad we ain't relying on your tracking methods.'

Clifford narrowed his eyes. 'What's that supposed to mean?'

'It means that Jim Stark told me where Kirk is, so tomorrow, I'll lead you to him.'

'Jim told you squat,' Clifford roared and turned. 'Don't push me, Spenser.'

Clifford hunkered down beside the campfire and warmed his hands, letting just enough of his irritation slip away.

6

In the morning the group set off two hours before dawn, heading north.

Clifford ignored last night's incident and didn't ask Spenser where to go, and Spenser didn't volunteer anything. Although Clifford still glared at Spenser's back as they rode, something about his hunched stance was more determined than before.

When first light arrived they cut across country, avoiding the trading post, and rejoined the western trail after a few miles.

Later in the morning Nat rode up to join Clifford and nodded back along the trail.

A new rider was following them.

They'd met few travellers in the journey, so from under the brim of his hat, Nat watched the portly man approach.

'He's Jim Stark,' Clifford said as the rider

closed. 'Spenser spoke to him at the poker game last night. He's Spenser's friend.'

Bill snorted and Nat nodded.

Jim Stark slowed to a steady trot and pulled alongside.

'You mind if I join you?' Jim asked, his voice light and cheerful.

Clifford shrugged. 'If'n you're heading in our direction, you can ride with us.'

'Much obliged.'

'And in what direction are you heading?'

'That-a-way,' Jim said waving a hand at the trail ahead.

Clifford grunted and pulled back to keep Jim and Spenser before him. He glanced at Nat and Bill, holding their gaze.

Both men turned to glare at Jim's back.

Jim and Spenser shared a few words and they rode in silence for the rest of the morning.

In the early afternoon they camped down in a clearing fifty yards from the trail to eat their provisions. Jim sat apart from the group, eating his own food.

When Spenser had chewed through a heel of bread, he strolled from Clifford and stared at Jim.

'So, Jim,' Spenser said, 'you didn't say before where you was heading.'

'I didn't,' Jim said through a mouthful of salted beef. 'My plans are kind of flexible.'

'Ours ain't. We know where we're heading.'

Jim shrugged. 'It's good for a man to know where he's heading.'

'Except our plans might not be the same as yours.'

'Like I say, I'm flexible, and while we're heading in the same direction, we can offer each other protection.' With his chin raised, Jim glanced at the surrounding hills and lowered his voice. 'You hear that there's all sorts out on the trail in these parts.'

'We're safe enough without you. Only person gaining is you.'

'Another gun is helpful,' Jim said, patting his gunbelt, 'especially as you ain't packing one these days.'

Spenser nodded. He glanced away and Jim returned to eating his beef. Then with his shoulder down, Spenser charged at Jim, knocking him on his back. On the ground they tumbled over, both arms wrapped around each other.

In a sudden movement, Clifford drew his gun and nodded to Nat to do the same. Both men kept their guns trained on the fighting twosome.

With a lunge, Jim clubbed Spenser away. Then Spenser rolled to his feet and backed a pace.

'What you do that for?' Jim shouted.

Spenser shrugged. 'You know.'

With a scything motion, Spenser kicked out at Jim's legs, tumbling him over, and leapt on his chest pinning him to the ground. With Jim's arms trapped, Spenser grabbed Jim's gun, swinging it round.

'That's as far as you go,' Clifford roared, holding his gun at arm's length. 'That gun goes straight to ground or your life ends.'

'It will go to ground,' Spenser said, 'as

soon as I've done this.' Spenser fired down at Jim, shooting him through the forehead. Then he hurled the gun from him and rolled to his feet, his hands held aloft.

Clifford stared at Spenser and then gestured to Nat to pick up the gun.

When Nat had taken the gun, Clifford placed a foot on a rock and shrugged.

'Why did you do that?'

'Ain't trusting Jim one bit. His sort has a big mouth. He ain't the sort of man we want with us.'

'How did you figure that out?'

'After he told me last night where Kirk is, he must have decided something. I ain't sure what it was but we didn't need to find out.'

'He didn't tell you where Kirk is,' Clifford roared, shaking his head. 'You ain't with us to think, just to help us find Kirk.'

'Maybe, but I reckon Jim is just the first sign of trouble.'

Spenser nodded along the trail. Everyone turned. Three hundred yards away a line of riders approached.

Clifford stalked round to join Nat and Bill.

'What do you reckon?'

Nat watched the riders and shrugged. 'I reckon Spenser probably had a point about that Jim, but we shouldn't worry about every person we meet on the trail.'

Clifford nodded and holstered his gun. 'Agreed. There's no reason to panic.' He waved an arm at Nat and pointed to the bushes. 'Hide that body. When those riders have passed, we'll bury it.'

Nat nodded. 'Sure.'

'And when he's buried I'll discuss this further with Spenser.'

Spenser glanced at the riders who were almost close enough to discern features.

'You sure this ain't the time to start panicking?' Spenser asked.

'I'm sure,' Clifford said. 'But you need to worry about what happens if you don't do what I tell you to do.'

Spenser helped Nat drag Jim's body

behind a bush, although their movements would be obvious to the riders if they were interested in them. Then they stood beside Jim's horse and watched the riders trot closer.

Nat gulped and dashed to Clifford, drawing his gun as he ran.

'What's wrong?' Clifford shouted.

'Those men,' Nat shouted. 'They're from the trading post.'

Clifford narrowed his eyes and then his hand whirled down to his gun. The four approaching riders were men they'd bested yesterday.

As Bill pulled his gun, Spenser nodded at the second gun that Nat held.

'Reckon as this is the time you let me defend myself,' Spenser said.

Nat glanced at Clifford but Clifford shook his head.

'Nope,' Clifford muttered. 'I ain't convinced where you'll fire and I ain't convinced these men want trouble.'

Fifty yards down the trail the men arced to

the side and fanned out to storm their campsite.

Clifford sighed. 'I am now.'

With no protection and no time to go for their horses, Bill, Nat and Clifford hunkered down in a line, their guns held out straight.

Spenser dashed behind Nat and knelt, watching the approaching riders. 'You can trust me,' Spenser whispered to Nat. 'Concentrate on them.'

'Yeah,' Nat muttered, 'but you still ain't getting a gun.'

Nat holstered the second gun. He hunched his shoulders higher and ignored Spenser. He aimed at the rider furthest to the left and waited until he had a clear shot. But this man shot at Nat, the bullet ripping his hat from his head.

Abandoning his former resolve, Nat jumped to his feet and dashed sideways, figuring that it was safer to be a moving target.

Gunfire blasted around Nat and he skidded to a halt, firing up at the nearest rider as he hurtled towards him.

Nat's first and second shots were wild, but the rider hauled his horse around, the horse rearing. The other three riders slid to a halt too and laid down a ripping blast of gunfire across the campsite.

Taking his chance, Nat dashed to the horse and leapt up to pull down the rider.

The rider swung down his gun. But Nat gripped the man's arm and tugged him from his horse. The man slid and collapsed at his feet and Nat kicked him full in the face. The fellow fell back, his head catching his horse's front hoof with a glancing blow.

Nat reckoned that should finish him off and he spun round. Gunfire blasted nearby as Nat dashed around the horse.

The riders were on the ground and everyone was slugging it out. Each fight was one on one, even Spenser helping to defend the campsite.

Nat swung his gun back and forth, searching for a clear target. Finding none, he tucked his gun in his belt and dashed into the fray, whirling his fists.

The nearest man was fighting Bill and Nat dragged him away, clubbing him flat-handed across the chin. The attacker stumbled away and Bill punched him deep into the kidneys and then gripped both hands, bringing them down on his back.

As the man hit the ground, Nat swirled round. A bullet blasted by his face. Nat flinched. The man he'd pulled from his horse had recovered and stood, his arm held straight as he took more careful aim.

Nat leapt to the side, scrabbling for his gun as he hit the ground. More gunfire blasted, but as he rolled to his feet with his gun out, the man collapsed with at least two bullets in him. Further gunfire sounded behind him and he swirled round.

Spenser had taken a gun and had shot three men, leaving just the man Nat and Bill had knocked down.

With a casual smile, Spenser swung the gun round and shot this man too.

'That's it,' Clifford shouted, aiming his

gun at Spenser. 'Put down the gun, Spenser.'

Spenser sighed. 'You ain't sounding grateful after I saved our lives.'

Nat glanced down and confirmed the gun Spenser held had fallen from his belt while he fought. He raised his hands.

'We *are* grateful,' Nat said, 'except we'll be happier once you've put down that gun.'

Spenser shrugged and glanced at the gun. Then he underhanded it towards Clifford.

'Gun was out of bullets anyhow. They're in these people.'

As none of them wanted to thank Spenser, they dragged the bodies in silence to a few hundred yards from the trail. They lacked the energy to bury the bodies so they hid them in the bushes, by which time the men's horses had wandered away.

'You reckon that's the last of the surprises?' Nat asked when they'd returned to their camp.

Clifford rubbed his forehead and sighed.

'We need to look out for more, but...'

Clifford trailed off and glared at Spenser. 'Unless our new partner is telling us anything different.'

Spenser licked his lips. 'As you asked so nicely, I reckon Jim Stark panicked after he told me where Kirk is and he visited these men in the trading post. He found out about our interest and followed us, and they followed him.'

Clifford nodded. 'Sounds possible, but you keep saying Jim Stark told you where Kirk is. I didn't hear that.'

'Not my fault that you don't listen.'

'I do, but I didn't hear it.' Clifford narrowed his eyes. 'Did you have words with Jim in the poker game that I didn't hear?'

'Nope.'

'Then how did he tell you where Kirk is?'

Spenser laughed and tipped back his hat.

'You ain't as suited to this line of work as you think you are. I'm much better at bounty hunting. Jim told me exactly where Kirk is.'

'All Jim said about Kirk is that he hadn't

heard about him for a while.'

Spenser grinned.

With a slow widening of his lips, Clifford matched the grin. He gestured to the horses and Spenser wandered to his, Clifford following.

'What?' Nat said. 'I don't get that. You understand what Spenser is saying?'

'Sure do.' Clifford said, mounting his horse. 'Jim hadn't heard about Kirk for a while. That means he's lying low in a hideout somewhere that nobody knows about. Except Spenser knows where it is.'

Nat nodded and mounted his horse.

'Which way, Mr Ten Per Cent?' Clifford asked.

With a smile, Spenser gestured west and they lined up to follow him.

7

For five days the group followed the trail as it turned north. They left the prairies far behind as the land became barren and harsh. Parched rocks and craggy hills surrounded them with no signs of life, either human or animal.

Early on the sixth day after their meeting with the men from the trading post, Spenser stopped. He glanced around at the surrounding hills and mopped his brow.

'We getting close?' Clifford asked.

'Yup.'

'Where now?'

Spenser shrugged. 'Kind of depends.'

'On what?' Clifford said, his voice low.

'On what we decide my terms for helping you are.'

Clifford spat on the ground. 'We don't

need that discussion again.'

'Yeah, but as we're close to Kirk's hideout, I'm thinking about the risks I'm taking.'

Clifford edged his horse closer to Spenser. 'As a dead man you ain't taking risks.'

Spenser shrugged. 'That's as maybe, but I got my demands. If you ignore them, you could spend the rest of your life wandering around these hills and never find where Kirk is hiding, until he finds you.'

Clifford took a deep breath. 'For the sake of peace, let's hear it.'

'I want a gun.'

'A gun!' Clifford roared, his voice echoing in the nearby hills. 'No way.'

Spenser turned from the hills and stared at Clifford.

'I ain't riding into Kirk's hideout without a gun. Unless we're lucky, some of us ain't coming out of there, and I want to be one of the lucky ones.' As Clifford continued to glare at him, Spenser shrugged. 'I took a gun twice back down the trail and both times I fired it at men who were against us.

I could have fired at you but I didn't.'

'If you had, you'd be dead.'

'Maybe, but I didn't, and that says you ought to trust me.'

Clifford sighed and glanced at Nat, who nodded.

'I reckon you're speaking enough sense. All right, you get a gun.'

Clifford slipped a spare gunbelt from his saddlebag. He glared at it a moment, and then with a shrug threw it to Spenser.

Spenser caught the gunbelt and slipped it around his waist. He smiled.

'Much obliged.'

'You got a gun,' Clifford muttered. 'Now lead us to Kirk or you'll get a chance to use it sooner than you'd planned.'

Spenser shrugged. 'I ain't finished demanding.'

Clifford took long deep breaths. 'Go on. What else you wanting?'

'Twenty per cent.'

With a great roar, Clifford threw back his head and laughed. When he stopped, he was still smiling.

'You ain't getting that.'

'Good,' Nat muttered, slipping his horse closer to them. 'I ain't happy with you giving Spenser ten per cent, but twenty per cent is too much. If you let him have that, it's coming out of your share.'

Bill grunted something indistinct under his breath.

Clifford nodded. 'My young friend is talking a lot of sense. You've pushed your luck too far.'

'Six hundred dollars ain't enough for what I'm about to do to Kirk,' Spenser said. 'Over a thousand dollars will be.'

Clifford grinned and patted his chin. 'I ain't got a problem with you asking.'

'I have,' Nat muttered.

Clifford lifted a hand. 'Let me finish. Are you interested in negotiation, Spenser?'

Spenser narrowed his deep-set eyes to lines. 'Depends.'

'It doesn't. My offer is worth more than you can believe. If you could imagine it, you'd know how good it is.'

'Go on.'

Clifford edged his horse to stand alongside Spenser.

'I'll give you twenty per cent of Kirk's bounty less your expenses.'

Nat snorted and edged away, shaking his head.

Spenser glanced at Nat, his brow furrowed. 'What expenses?'

'If you're a part of this team,' Clifford said, 'you should pay for your own expenses.'

'Probably. But they must be small.'

Clifford grinned. 'Your expenses came to six hundred dollars. So twenty per cent of the bounty less expenses means you still get six hundred dollars.'

Spenser reached under his hat to scratch his head.

'You saying the bribes to get me out of jail cost six hundred dollars?'

'Yup. Except the terms of your release make it such a good offer. You see. You're dead.'

'Jim Stark said that about me too,' Spenser said, his voice low.

'He said that because you *are* dead. The authorities hung you in Beaver Ridge jail last week.'

Spenser glanced at Bill, who grinned, and at Nat, who glanced away to rub a hand over the back of his neck.

'I don't feel hung.'

'Yeah, that's because the body on the end of the rope was another lowlife, Sam Taylor, whom I dragged in. Sam was worth three hundred dollars dead or alive, except Sam was alive when I handed him over. Certain friends at Beaver Ridge jail certified that he was dead, which he is now as those certain friends also certified that his name was Spenser O'Connor and hung him in your place.'

Spenser rocked his head from side to side.

'Then they're a body short. How did they cover up that?'

Clifford chuckled. 'I can see you have a devious mind, but I reckon six hundred dollars solved that problem.'

'Why should that encourage me to go against Kirk?'

'Because you're officially dead. You may not have a pardon but you're of no interest to the authorities. For a man like you, that has to be worth more than money.'

Spenser whistled through his teeth. 'You're probably right.'

'Do we have a deal? It cost me six hundred dollars to buy your faked death. It's only fair that comes out of your cut. So, you'll come out of this with six hundred dollars and a chance to start again as someone else.'

Spenser tipped back his hat and lifted the reins.

'Deal.'

Without further word, Spenser swung his horse from the trail and headed towards a long rock-filled gully.

With a shared glance, the others followed.

Clifford hung back to glare at Nat.

'You do remember,' Clifford said, his voice low, 'that whatever I offer Spenser, the only cut he's getting will be from Bill's knife?'

Nat sighed. 'Suppose so. I just hate this double-dealing. To my mind, if we make a deal with someone, we stick with it.'

Clifford shrugged and hurried after Spenser.

For the rest of the morning they headed up the gully, the terrain becoming craggier with each passing mile. When the gully finished, they reached a wide plateau, but ahead more gullies and crags headed higher into the hills.

They rode in twos, Nat riding with Spenser as they picked a route between the rocks.

'How much further?' Nat asked, mopping his brow.

'Not much,' Spenser said.

'The riding get any easier?'

'Nope.'

'Why hide out in such a place?'

Spenser smiled and stared ahead.

Nat shrugged. 'All right. I got the idea. You want to be quiet.'

Spenser coughed. 'Nope. Keep talking to me, Nat, as much as you like.'

'Why? You ain't interested in talking about anything.'

'True, but people are watching us. If we're talking we are showing we're unconcerned.'

Nat gulped, but resisted the urge to peer around in all directions. 'Tell me where these people who are watching us are hiding.'

Spenser shrugged. 'Won't do you any good. The hiding places change each time, but wherever they are, they've got a good position and it's one we won't force them out of.'

'We should let the others know.'

'If they know, it ain't doing them any good and if they don't know, knowing won't help them.'

'That ain't sounding good.'

'Nope. A frontal attack won't force Kirk from his hideout. We need to get in and take our chances, and that means following the entry rules.'

In a sudden lurch, Spenser drew his horse

to a halt and held up a hand.

Clifford and Bill drew alongside.

'What you doing, Spenser?' Clifford muttered.

'I'm waiting.'

'We're being watched,' Nat whispered.

'I know that,' Clifford snapped. 'Just want to know what Spenser is doing.'

Spenser dropped his hand and sighed.

'Know you'll hate this, but this is where you put all your trust in me.'

Clifford chuckled. 'I don't trust you at all.'

'You got no choice.'

Clifford glanced at the barren rocks that surrounded them and mopped the back of his neck.

'See your point, but remember this – the second something goes wrong, you're the first to die.'

'It won't go wrong if you trust me.' Spenser nodded forward to where, from the tumble of rocks, a long-coated man had appeared.

The man cocked his battered hat low and

sauntered through the rocks. Nat glanced around searching for where the other men, who must have rifles on them, might be hiding. He only saw rocks.

Twenty yards away the man stopped and rested his rifle on his hip. 'Howdy, Spenser,' the man shouted.

'Howdy to you, Ned.'

The man, Ned, nodded and wandered a pace closer.

'Never thought you'd return here. When you left, you said you were striking out on your own. Guessing as you is in a lot of trouble.'

Spenser edged his horse forward. 'You'd think so, but the story is a whole lot more complicated than that.'

Ned smiled. 'Kind of like to hear that story.'

'And I'd like to tell it to you.'

Ned gestured with his rifle over Spenser's shoulder. 'These your friends?'

'Yup. They helped me out when I was in a mighty tricky situation. We're a team.'

Ned stood to one side. He waved a hand over his head and sauntered to his rock. He ducked and disappeared from sight, the surrounding barren rocks returning to their seemingly unpopulated state.

In the baking sun they waited for ten minutes. As the waiting dragged on Nat's nerves, he edged forward to Spenser's side.

'How much longer are we waiting?' he whispered.

'As long as it takes.' Spenser ran a hand over his forehead. 'Be patient. We're waiting for the signals to reach Kirk. When Ned gets his answer he'll let us know.'

Spenser tapped his holster and smiled.

Nat sighed. 'Let's hope the answer is one we'll like to hear.'

They waited in silence, Nat gazing back and forth across the rocks without moving his head, searching for the flashes of light or whatever signals must be passing back to the hideout. He saw nothing.

Ned stood from his rock. He stared at them and then ducked.

'Come on,' Spenser said.

'That was the signal to go ahead?' Nat asked.

'I've taken it as that.' Spenser sighed. 'Anything else would have involved us being dead by now.'

With the route ahead becoming more treacherous, rocks sliding from under their horses' hoofs with each pace, they lined up to snake through the pass and into a wide gully beyond. The gully stretched on ahead into the hills and they followed it in silence.

Nat adopted a relaxed posture while examining each likely spot where someone could be hiding. But there were so many places. As soon as anyone started an ambush they faced a large disadvantage.

At the head of the gully, the land flattened letting them view the surrounding hills, the dust in the air shrouding their outlines, but on one side there was a further craggy hill, riddled with caves and fallen rocks.

Spenser swung his horse to face this craggy mass and halted. They drew alongside and stood in a line.

Clifford edged closer to Spenser. 'All right, Spenser. You've got us this far, but now the fun starts and you follow orders to the letter.'

Spenser lifted a hand and shook his head.

'I don't need threats and I don't need you dictating our plans. We do this my way, if we want to live.'

'You ain't giving orders.' Clifford gritted his teeth and spat on the ground. He rubbed his chin and sighed. 'But I'm willing to listen to ideas as to our plans.'

Spenser laughed, the sound low. 'This is my idea. Kirk has between fifteen and twenty men here. Three or four will be hidden along our route in. It's the only way out. All other sides of this plateau lead to a long drop and death. So if we leave in a hurry, we keep our heads down and bolt for freedom. Some of us might avoid the gunshots.'

'We ain't leaving. I'm only interested in ideas to get us in the hideout.'

Spenser nodded. 'I know. More rifles are on us here and we won't get a clean shot at their owners. Our only hope is to head into the pass on the left of the crag. When we're face to face we have a chance. It ain't much of one, but it's a chance.'

With a slow nod, Clifford sighed. 'All right. That sounds like enough information. I'll give the word and we'll go for it.'

'You won't give the word. Someone will come out to see me. I'll go with him and when I've convinced Kirk you're trustworthy, he'll let you enter.' As Clifford grunted an oath, Spenser lifted a hand. 'Don't say that if I try anything I'm dead. It ain't worth it. If I tell Kirk who you are, he'll kill me in a heartbeat and you'll be dead a few seconds after that.'

Clifford sighed. He glanced at Nat and Bill who both nodded. Clifford sighed again.

'All right. I never thought I'd say it, but I'll trust you. What's our best chance?'

Spenser licked his lips as a lone rider

trotted from the crag and approached them.

'Once you've rounded the crag, you'll see a cave up the hillside. That's Kirk's base. If we wait until he takes us in there, he'll have us trapped from behind and in front and we ain't got a chance. So we wait until we're half-way between the cave and the crag, by then Kirk will be confident we're trustworthy and his men will relax. Then we go for it. I'll give the signal and you take as many of his men as you can, then head for the rocks on the right. There's plenty of hiding there.'

'And then?'

'We pick off anybody outside and set in for a long fight against those in the cave.'

With the approaching man having reached them, Clifford nodded. Spenser rode forward to the new man. They spoke in low tones and then headed for the crag.

Nat shuffled closer to Clifford.

'Seems as it's up to Spenser now,' Nat muttered.

'Yeah,' Clifford said with a sigh. 'Let's hope I was right in trusting him.'

Nat shook his head. 'Hate the sound of that.'

'Don't worry,' Clifford muttered from the corner of his mouth. 'Spenser's got us this far, but from now on, I'm in control. I'm giving the signal to attack, not him.'

Clifford patted his holster and Bill patted his holster in reply.

Nat nodded and hunched over his horse, watching Spenser disappear around the side of the crag.

8

In pensive silence Clifford, Nat and Bill waited for long minutes on the plateau, each second dragging on them.

Nat patted his thigh. His neck itched as if someone had a rifle aimed there, but he kept his head still as he stared at the rocks ahead, searching for the hidden gunmen.

When the waiting had caused Nat's guts to rumble, a lone man stood on the crag, waved, and then disappeared again.

Nat turned to Clifford.

'Guessing as that's all we'll get,' Nat said with a sigh.

Clifford nodded. 'You ready?'

'As I'll ever be.'

With a short nod from Bill, they headed in a line towards the crag, their horses clumping across the hard ground.

Moving with steady care through the tumble of rocks, they edged around the crag and the gully beyond opened to them, revealing a terrain as Spenser had described it.

Nat glared at the barren rocks, searching for gunmen and good places to hide when their ambush started.

Huge boulders were on either side of the gully but the ones on the right were larger and would provide better cover. At the end of the gully was a large cave, fallen boulders partially blocking its entrance.

'So far, so good,' Clifford whispered.

As they trotted from the gully, dirty, hard-boned men appeared one by one from behind the rocks. They sauntered round to face them with their hats pulled low and their long coats rippling in the warm, dust-filled breeze.

Nat counted seven men and one of them was Spenser O'Connor but despite gazing at each man, Nat didn't recognize Kirk Morton, although he'd only seen a poster likeness.

One man paced from the group and lifted a foot on to a small rock. With the barrel of his gun, he tipped back his hat and grinned, his weather-hardened face creasing in the grime.

'That's far enough,' he shouted.

Without looking at each other, Nat and the rest halted.

Spenser wandered round in an arc to stand ten yards to the group's left.

'You can trust these men,' he shouted. 'They'll be fine additions.'

Kirk's men stared in silence. The only sound was the breeze whistling through the rocks.

'Yeah,' Clifford shouted, his voice loud as it cut through the quiet. 'You got nothing to fear from us. Spenser's a good friend of ours and any friend of Spenser's is a friend of ours too.'

The nearest man spat on the ground at his feet.

'That's mighty friendly,' he muttered.

'We're mighty friendly people.'

The man edged down his hat further, hiding his eyes.

'Only Kirk can work that out.'

'Then lead us to him and we'll talk.'

From beneath the hat, the man grinned and paced to the side.

To a short waved gesture, Clifford and his group dismounted and stalked around from their horses. Then they threw down their guns.

With a series of glances between themselves, Kirk's men edged to the cave entrance, their long coats pressed flat against their backs.

Clifford produced another gun from his jacket. He swung his gun up and around, aiming towards the men.

Taking this as their cue, Nat and Bill leapt for their guns as Clifford sprayed an arc of bullets across the men's chests.

Half of the men fell in the initial onslaught. Nat gritted his teeth against shooting any man in cold blood, but before he chided himself, the surviving men splayed bullets back.

In self-preservation, Nat dived to the side. He rolled twice and came up running for the boulders. Bullets peppered around him as he dived behind the nearest boulder, rolling to a standstill.

Bill and Clifford arrived seconds later and swung down beside him.

'We got this far,' Nat muttered, 'and we're still alive.'

Bill laughed. 'You sound surprised.'

'Yeah, despite what he said, I expected

Spenser to double-cross us.'

Clifford snorted. 'Save that opinion until we get proof. Spenser didn't fire at Kirk's men.'

In a sudden gesture, Clifford glanced over the top of the boulder and ducked.

'What did you see?' Nat asked as he reloaded.

'Three bodies are out there. The rest have hightailed it into the cave.'

'Any sign of Spenser?'

'Nope. He must be hiding out there somewhere.'

Nat crawled around the side of the boulder for a better view of the terrain. He lay on his belly and gazed left and right.

The cave was about eighty yards away and ten yards higher than their hiding-place. He rolled over to look up at the tumble of rocks above him searching for a better hiding-place. If they were higher, they'd look down into the cave and have a better chance of picking off the outlaws inside.

A gunshot slammed into the boulder

inches from Nat's face, the shards of rock peppering his cheek. Nat hit the ground and, crawling on his belly, dashed back behind the boulder.

More gunfire blasted into the boulder and it was all on the side on which they were hiding. Nat glanced up. Bill and Clifford had hit the ground and were flat out.

Nat crawled to them. 'Where's this shooting coming from?'

'Don't know for sure,' Clifford said, 'but I reckon as the men who watched us come into the hideout followed us and are now on our side of the gully.'

Nat glanced up, but Clifford slammed a firm hand on his head, pressing his face into the dirt.

Another round of gunfire blasted into the boulder only inches above Nat's head.

Nat waited until the gunfire ended. Then he rolled as far into the rocks at his back as he could. Still keeping his head down, he glanced up, only seeing the closest rocks, but that meant whoever was firing couldn't see him.

'They've got us pinned down,' he muttered.

'Yeah,' Clifford said. 'Worse, we're relying on Spenser to get us out of here.'

'Let's hope we had him all wrong.' Nat rubbed his neck. 'He ain't double-crossed us, but we don't know yet whether he's helping us has or preserved his own worthless hide and ran.'

Clifford sighed. 'I ain't holding out much hope.'

With them pinned down, Nat searched along their small expanse of space, looking for an escape route or a way to make a stand. But other than jumping up and hoping to hit their well-hidden assailants before they blasted back at them, he saw no options.

For five minutes they waited. Then Clifford crawled to Nat.

'Forget Spenser picking off those men. There is another route out of here and he's run. With us pinned down, they'll try to force us out of here before too much longer and I ain't fancying our chances.'

Nat rubbed his forehead. Then in a lithe movement he leapt to his feet. He glanced over the boulder they were hiding behind and then leapt to the ground as gunfire erupted around him.

'You're right,' he said. 'Kirk's men are in the cave entrance. They'll be sneaking down towards us any minute.'

'Right,' Clifford muttered. 'It's now or never.'

Shuffling on his elbows, Bill slipped along the ground to their sides.

'We go for the horses?' Bill asked.

'Nope. They ain't out there so I reckon they've wandered off. We go for whoever's got a drop on us. Then we head for the cave. Bill, go left. Nat, go right. I'll head up the centre.'

Nat glanced at Bill and nodded.

In a line, they shuffled as far round the boulder as possible without being seen from above. Then on the count of three, they leapt to their feet and dashed from the boulder.

With his head low, Nat dashed along the base of the crag away from the cave, ignoring how Clifford and Bill fared. Sporadic gunfire blasted around him, but as soon as he saw a gap in the boulders he leapt into the space and paused for breath.

From further round the crag more gunfire sounded.

Nat took a deep breath and headed up the crag. He'd been lucky to find a route that was closed in on both sides, but that also meant he couldn't see what was happening. He scrambled on hands and feet over the rocks, his boots slipping on the large rocks, but once he'd climbed over the first dozen boulders, the route flattened.

Nat knelt and craned his neck to judge his position.

A man leapt out from the boulder before him, his clawed swipe of his arms wrapping Nat in a bear hug.

Nat gasped as the air blasted from his

lungs and he fell, landing heavily on his back. His gun flew from his hand and unable to stop his movement, he slid back, heading down the smooth boulder head first.

He threw out his arms, desperate for purchase, the ground at the bottom of the boulder closing with increasing speed. He slammed his eyes shut and then they landed, to lie in a tangle at the bottom of the boulder.

Nat staggered free of his assailant and searched for his gun, seeing nothing.

His assailant staggered to his feet, shaking his head and, with the slow movements of a winded person, he grabbed his gun and lifted it.

Nat kicked away the gun and swung round, clubbing the man with a solid blow to the jaw.

The man toppled to the side. He fell over a boulder and slid to the bottom. This time, his desperate flailing of arms didn't slow his descent and he rolled over the next boulder.

He cried out, the sound dying as he tumbled again, his speed increasing with each bounce over the tangle of boulders.

Long before the man reached the bottom of the crag, Nat turned and searched for his gun. When he found it, he shook his head and headed up the crag, this time glaring at each boulder he passed.

He scrambled over another boulder and the crag flattened into a wide mass of rocks.

Ahead, four men were hunkered down behind a large flat rock and were firing down the other side of the crag. Between the gunshots, somebody returned fire.

Edging forward on tiptoes, Nat snaked between the rocks getting as close to them as possible without them seeing him. At thirty yards away he slipped down between two boulders. He glanced around, ensuring that nobody else was on top of the crag and took careful aim at a man in the middle.

Nat fired, the man tumbling over. Then he fired across the other men, each man leaping to the ground. He fell back behind his boulder. With practised dexterity, he reloaded and then glanced up.

Three men charged at him with guns brandished, splattering gunfire. Nat dropped, searching for other good hiding-places. Seeing none, he leapt to his feet, the men just yards away. He fired twice, one man collapsing, and dashed to his side. Gunfire sounded and he slid to a halt, but as he turned on the hip, the two remaining men fell on to their fronts.

With a long sigh, Nat wiped his brow and nodded to Clifford and Bill, who had climbed over the edge of the crag.

He checked the men were dead and dashed across the crag top to join his partners.

'Mighty glad to see you,' Nat said. 'We've got a good position.'

Clifford grinned, but his grin died as soon as it appeared.

'Only if we can hold it.'

Nat spun round.

A line of men charged over the edge of the

crag, laying down a peppering of gunfire.

Nat gritted his teeth and charged them, snaking left and right as he ran, and avoiding firing until the last possible moment. From the corner of his eye, he saw Bill collapse and then he was within ten yards of Kirk's men. He fired in an arc across the men, still running.

With Clifford joining him in the gunfire, most of the outlaws fell, but with his gun empty, Nat had no choice but to leap at the nearest standing man and club him to the ground.

Another man appeared from behind the first and aimed a huge kick at Nat's legs.

Nat swung to the side, missing the kick and weighing in with his fists flying.

With the gunfire having ceased, the fighting was with fists alone.

Nat gulped as six other men climbed over the side of the crag and joined their colleagues. He leapt to the side and threw his assailant to the ground. Then he charged another man, but this fellow shrugged off

Nat's blows and clamped a firm grip around his chest.

From behind a fist thumped into Nat's kidneys and he collapsed, a boot slamming into his chin as he fell. He rolled away, missing a few kicks but getting others along the length of his body.

He rolled free from the tangle of assailants and staggered to his feet.

Ten yards away Clifford had his knife pulled, but a large man kicked it from his hand and, within seconds, three more men leapt on him and pummelled him to the ground.

More men formed a circle, surrounding Nat. Each man had a lively grin and his fists raised. As one they took a short pace in to Nat.

With the back of his hand, Nat rubbed his mouth, searching for an opening.

'Come on,' Nat shouted, beckoning them on with his fists. 'What're you waiting for?'

'They're waiting for me,' a calm voice said from outside the circle. The circle of men parted.

A new man strode into the centre of the group. Beneath his long coat, this man's clothing was neat, twin guns nestled on his hips and his eyes were cold enough to chill Nat in the heat of the afternoon.

'I'm guessing you're Kirk Morton,' Nat said with a gulp.

'You're right at that.' Kirk turned to look over the edge of the crag. He glanced at the surrounding hills and clicked his fingers. 'Take them alive. I'm in the mood for entertainment.'

9

Nat gulped as Kirk Morton edged the knife towards his face.

'You got no reason to do that,' Nat muttered, unable to stop his voice from shaking.

Kirk sighed and glanced at the knife. The knife reflected the faint light from outside the cave into Nat's eyes.

'An interesting theory,' Kirk said, 'and you're right, but you don't know what I'm about to do. Would you like to guess?'

Nat glanced around. On all sides, Kirk's men sat in a circle with their mouths open in wide grins. Nat counted fourteen.

Six feet to his side, Clifford glared at Kirk, but Bill had his head hung, the blood from the bullet-nick along his chest bathing his clothes red.

For what Nat hoped was the last time, he flexed his wrists above his head, but found no give in the rope that suspended him from the top of the stake.

'I ain't guessing,' Nat muttered.

'You should. Many people have guessed what I'll do to them. They are always wrong.' Kirk grinned and threw the knife from hand to hand. 'What I do is much worse than they can imagine.'

'Get to it. Listening to you whine is the

worst thing I can imagine.'

'You have spirit,' Kirk said, his voice staying at the same low level. 'I like that. It'll take more skill to rip that out of you.'

Kirk edged closer, walking sideways, the knife held before him. Kirk's grin was wide, his eyes cold, reflective surfaces. Moving with extreme slowness he dangled the knife in towards Nat's face.

Although he tried not to, Nat watched the knife slip closer and closer until the point pressed against his chin.

He flinched, the cold deeper than he expected. The knife's point pressed into his flesh and grated to the side. Warmth gushed down his neck, with a short stabbing pain.

'That wasn't too bad, was it?' Kirk said, his grinning face inches from Nat.

'Seeing your ugly face is worse.'

Kirk chuckled, the sound chilling Nat more than looking into his eyes.

'Trying to rile me into killing you will fail. I'll work all the slower.' Kirk withdrew the knife and glared at the blood dripping from the blade. 'Perhaps I'll let you watch me do the others first – it looks as if I've already started on one of them. And all the time you'll know I'm saving the worst for you.'

Nat chewed, working up enough moisture to spit into Kirk's face. A gunshot echoed outside the cave.

Kirk glanced around.

A second gunshot sounded, this time closer. 'Where's that coming from?' Kirk shouted.

Kirk tucked the knife into his belt and swirled round, pulling his twin guns. He stalked to the cave entrance. A gunshot cannoned into the cave wall and he ducked and backed a pace. He ordered two men outside and slipped along the wall to Nat.

'You know what this is about?' he asked.

Nat shook his head. 'Nope. We came on our own.'

'What about Spenser O'Connor?'

'He ran, like all you dogs do when there's trouble.'

'So you reckon it's someone else?'

'Yeah. Spenser hasn't the guts to attack you.'

Kirk nodded as a rapid series of gunshots blasted into the cave.

'I reckon as you're right unless Spenser's got himself a whole lot of courage and a whole new rapid way of firing.'

'Why not go outside and see who it is?'

Kirk chuckled. 'You know that I'll get the truth from you.'

'You got it,' Nat said with an involuntary gulp. 'I don't know who's attacking you. We came with Spenser O'Connor and nobody else.'

Kirk shrugged, his knife slipping from his belt.

'Ain't got the time to test that. When we've captured your friends, I'll be asking you plenty of questions.'

As Kirk wandered to the cave entrance, Nat gulped and glanced at Clifford.

'Spenser,' Nat mouthed. 'Surely not.'

Clifford shrugged as much as his bonds let him.

At the cave entrance, Kirk barked instructions to his men and they fanned out, taking positions behind each available rock.

From inside, Nat saw that this cave was an excellent defensive position, and if the attacker were Spenser, he'd need an inspired plan to succeed.

With a shrug of his shoulders, Nat stretched his bonds to their limit, but found no give. Then something glinted in the corner of his eye. He closed his eyes, hoping that he was right, and glanced down.

Kirk's knife had fallen at Nat's feet as he'd returned to the cave entrance.

Nat stretched out his right foot. He slammed it on the knife and, with the heel of his boot, he dragged it in towards him. He levered the knife up on to the top of his boot and glared down at it.

Clifford sighed. 'So near and yet so far.'

Nat nodded. 'You got any ideas?'

'Nope. Not unless you're double-jointed or got a third hand I ain't seen before.'

Nat laughed, the sound hollow, and

without much hope, he trapped the knife between his feet and braced his back. He swung his feet from the ground and upwards as high as he could.

With his weight suspended from his shoulders, his arms creaked as if they were being torn from their sockets and, gritting his teeth against the pain, he only levered his feet to hip level.

'I ain't as limber as I thought,' Nat said with a sigh as he lowered his legs, ensuring he kept the knife gripped between his feet.

'Give up and put your hope in Spenser,' Bill said, lifting his head for the first time.

Nat snarled and, with an angry lunge, he swung up his feet as hard as he could. The effort produced a huge creaking from above and, for one terrible second, Nat thought he'd wrenched his arms from their sockets.

Then the stake holding him toppled over. Unable to stop himself, he tumbled face down in the dirt.

He lay winded. But he'd received the faint chance he'd hoped for, so he rolled over, still attached to the stake, and scrambled around on the ground for the knife.

'Quick,' Clifford muttered. 'To your left and down a bit.'

From the cave entrance footsteps sounded, and Nat thrust his questing hands in the direction Clifford indicated. He saw the knife and his hands closed on it. He turned in the knife, severing his bonds. In a tangle of cut rope, he rolled to his feet and turned.

One of Kirk's men stood twenty yards in from the entrance, shaking his head. He rubbed a hand over his shock of red hair. With slow, almost contemptuous ease, he lifted his gun and aimed it at Nat.

Nat had never thrown a knife, but with no choice, he underhanded it at the red-haired man.

The red-haired man danced to the side, although the knife was hurtling by him, but Nat hadn't put all his hope in the knife. As soon as it left his hand he followed through with a running dive at the man's legs.

The red-haired man fired down, the gunshot blasting past Nat's head and then Nat was on him, bundling him to the ground. The red-haired man fired a second time, the gunshot blasting uselessly into the cave roof, but Nat clubbed his fist into the man's face, a second blow following straight afterwards.

The red-haired man grunted and rolled on to his back.

Nat grabbed the man's gun and glanced up. Kirk and his men were firing at their attackers outside the cave. Nat scrambled for the knife and then dashed to Clifford and Bill, severing their bonds with quick swipes of the knife.

Both men rubbed their wrists as they stepped from the stakes and stared at the cave entrance.

'What you reckon we should do?' Bill asked, fingering the bullet nick on his chest.

Clifford shrugged. 'Don't care. We're free and I ain't being captured again. We either escape or die.'

Clifford glanced at Nat and Bill. They nodded.

Nat offered Clifford the gun.

'I'm better with a knife than you,' Clifford said, taking the knife instead.

As Nat nodded, a bullet ripped into the cave wall beside them, a second followed even closer. Nat swirled round.

Four men had given up on the fight at the cave entrance and had returned to see what was happening.

Nat fired at the first man. Then he swung round and dashed further into the cave.

Clifford prepared to throw the knife, but seeing he was alone, he dashed after Nat and Bill as they hurtled deeper into the cave.

Further gunshots blasted around them, but each shot ricocheted against the cave walls, sounding like a continual barrage of gunfire. With each dashed pace ahead, the cave closed in all directions.

'You got a plan?' Clifford shouted.

'Cave's got to go somewhere,' Nat

muttered with a glance over his shoulder at the men who chased after them.

'Who says it has to?'

Nat shrugged and then ducked as the cave ceiling sloped down faster than he expected. He dashed, doubled over, for five yards hoping the cave opened up again, but it closed down to a pile of wet rocks and a solid wall.

'That's the end of that,' Nat muttered and spun round.

Bill and Clifford had hunkered down behind a rock. Nat joined them.

'At least we got a good place to defend,' Bill said with a sigh.

A man leapt over the rock at them, bundling Bill to the ground. Clifford leapt on this man's back, scything the knife at his neck, but a second man followed around the rock, his gun blasting a bullet inches from Clifford's face.

From scant feet away, Nat swung the gun up, firing into the man, who fell against the rock and rolled back to topple on him. Nat floundered under the fallen body. Then bullets ripped into the body as the last two men dashed round the rock and stood over him.

With no hope of aiming, Nat fired and fired until his finger's twitching produced a dull thudding sound. Then he hurled the body from him and leapt to his feet, swirling his fists in the hope of getting in a blow before they finished him. But their attackers were dead at his feet. Clifford reached down and slipped the knife from one body's belly. He wiped the knife on his sleeve and pulled Bill to his feet from under the final body.

Bill was drenched in blood, but most came from his assailant's slashed throat.

'Told you this was the best way to go,' Nat said.

Clifford laughed. He unhooked the first body's gunbelt, passed it to Bill, and unhooked the other belts.

'I'll give you that,' Clifford said, 'but escaping to nowhere was easy. Now comes the difficult part.'

When they each had a gun, they stalked through the cave, heading for the entrance.

From ahead, rapid gunfire echoed.

'If that's Spenser outside,' Nat said, 'I'll hug his scrawny hide.'

'I might join you,' Clifford muttered. 'But it ain't him.'

'Then who's attacking them?'

'I've seen no sign of anyone following us, but with a bounty of six thousand dollars on Kirk, it has to be possible.'

They edged around the last bend in the cave to return to the main entrance area and arrived as quiet descended on the cave. Scattered across the entrance were the bodies of over a dozen men.

Nat counted through the men they'd killed and even with Spenser's high estimate of the number of outlaws here, most of Kirk's men were dead. Then a lone figure dashed into the cave.

Nat recognized Kirk Morton. He aimed at him but didn't fire when he saw that Kirk wasn't packing a gun.

Kirk glared at them and kicked at a stone. He folded his arms and stood straight, his eyes bright and a small smile on his face.

Clifford stalked forward, with his gun aimed at Kirk's forehead. 'It looks like you're mine, Kirk Morton.'

'He ain't,' a voice shouted from outside the cave.

They looked up.

The jailer from Beaver Ridge jail, Rory Johnson, sauntered into the cave with his gun aimed at Kirk's back. Behind him a steady stream of men arrived, all grizzled and hard.

Nat counted twelve men, and he recognized some as other jailers from Beaver Ridge jail.

Clifford glanced at Kirk and sighed.

'Being as I had help – *we* have got you.'

'Yeah,' Rory said, 'I suppose *we* have.'

Still with his gun on Kirk, Clifford shrugged.

'Never realized that you followed us.'

Rory laughed. 'Suppose you bounty

hunters are good at tracking but not so good at looking over their shoulders. I've been following you from the jail. It was easy. I followed the trail of bodies.'

'So you're tired of being a jailer?'

'Jailing got tired of me, but I have what I came here for.' Rory gazed at Kirk, looking from his head to his boots. 'This him? He ain't looking like six thousand dollars' worth of trouble.'

'He doesn't,' Nat said, fingering the cut on his chin. 'But when he has a knife pressed against you, he's worth that.'

Rory shrugged. 'Even so, if'n he'd stayed in here, we'd have had no chance of getting him. But his men all charged out of the cave and they were easy pickings. I'm reckoning he ain't much of a leader.'

Clifford nodded. 'Hot blood gets them all in the end.'

Clifford wandered to the stakes and unhooked the length of rope he'd previously had around his own hands. While Rory kept his gun on Kirk, he tied Kirk's hands together and secured his arms to his sides. He pulled on the rope, ensuring the bonds were tight, and stood back.

Bill shuffled round to stare at Kirk.

'I've looked forward to this,' Bill whispered. 'I know most of your tricks and I'm looking forward to trying them out on you.'

Kirk spat at Bill.

'Easy,' Clifford said, 'you got plenty of time to enjoy yourself.'

Bill shrugged and strode back to Clifford. 'Sure,' he said, grinning. 'I got all the time I need.'

Clifford turned to Rory. 'We're much obliged to you for arriving while we have our skins on. Suppose in the circumstances I should change our financial arrangement.'

Rory grinned and tapped a finger against his chin.

'That's mighty generous of you. If I remember right you gave me three hundred dollars, and promised me the same again when you had the bounty.'

Clifford glanced at the circle of Rory's men.

'Perhaps that is a low return for what you and your colleagues did.' He rubbed his chin. 'I agreed to split the bounty with Nat, but I'll offer a fairer split of a third for Nat, a third for me, and a third for you.'

He glanced at Nat, who nodded.

'A whole third,' Rory said, his voice high and obviously faking amusement.

Nat guessed Clifford hadn't expected to leave with anything more than half of the bounty for himself and Nat and the other half for Rory, but having stated his offer, he couldn't back too fast.

Clifford took a deep breath. 'Yeah. That's the fairest division.'

'Perhaps it is for you, but I have a better idea.' Rory sighed, prolonging the moment. 'I'm offering three hundred dollars.'

'What's that supposed to...' Clifford trailed off and rubbed his forehead. 'You wouldn't.'

'Sure would. That's what you gave me to

free Spenser O'Connor.' Rory looked around. 'What happened to him? Anyhow, you can have that back.' Rory reached into his pocket and threw a wad of notes at Clifford's feet.

Clifford ignored the notes and glared at Rory. 'And the rest of the deal?'

'There ain't one. That's all you're getting.'

With his head thrust low, Clifford charged across the cave, heading for Rory, but a row of guns lifted from Rory's watching men. One man fired into the cave roof.'

Clifford slid to a stop, scant feet from Rory, his hands lifted and held as claws.

'You'd better be joking,' Clifford muttered.

'Why?' Rory said, smiling. 'The man who captures an outlaw deserves the bounty. That'd be me. But you know the rules of hunting for bounty and things don't always work out like that. The man who brings in the outlaw collects the bounty. But that'd be me too. Life ain't always fair but there it is.'

'We worked together on this. I found the hideout and removed all his guards.'

'From what I saw, I saved your lives. I could have waited until Kirk had carved you into pieces and fed you to the vultures but I didn't. I thought you'd be more grateful.'

'I ain't,' Clifford muttered.

'So what? As you're so ungrateful, you can walk to the nearest town. It's called Dust Creek, I believe. It ain't far. Perhaps after the walk you'll appreciate what I did for you.'

Clifford lifted his fist, ready to punch Rory in the guts, but Nat strode to him and slammed a hand on Clifford's elbow.

'Enough, Clifford. We're alive and I'm settling for that.'

Clifford glared at Rory and then turned.

'This ain't over,' he muttered.

Rory shrugged and with his men behind him he strode from the cave, Kirk clasped between two of his largest men.

When they'd gone, Nat edged to the cave entrance, confirming they rounded up all the remaining horses, but they threw three canteens of water and a small package of food on the ground.

Nat wandered into the cave and sighed. 'They've gone.'

'Yeah,' Clifford whispered, staring at the ground.

Bill patted Clifford on the shoulder.

'Come on,' Bill said. 'We ain't getting back at Rory by sitting here.'

Clifford grinned. 'Yeah, you're right.'

Nat glanced at the stakes and shivered.

'What we doing? It's a long way to Dust Creek.'

'Sure is,' Clifford muttered, 'and the sooner we set off the sooner we get there.'

'And the sooner we get Rory,' Bill said as they stormed outside.

10

Nat, Clifford and Bill walked through the long, hot day, heading from Kirk Morton's hideout to Dust Creek. They scrambled down the series of gullies following the same route by which they'd entered Kirk's hideout. Each step threw great gouts of dust into the air as they slipped down the rough rockstrewn path.

Late in the day they reached the main trail. They all hunched over and rested their hands on their knees as they caught their breath.

'You planning to get back Kirk?' Nat asked.

'You guessed it,' Clifford muttered and spat on the ground.

'Rory was right. He saved our lives. I'm grateful for that. We shouldn't repay him with whatever I'm sure you're planning.'

Clifford stared down the trail and then looked over his shoulder. Barren rocks faced him in both directions. He mopped his brow and sighed.

'Maybe, but that jailer double-crossed us and was always planning to double-cross us. Even when he took my money to free Spenser, he knew what he'd do. If we'd captured Kirk like we'd planned, he'd have tried to take him from us.'

'Probably,' Nat said, hating the sound of revenge for revenge's sake.

'No probably about it,' Bill muttered, lifting his hat to mop a hand across his ravaged face. 'Rory saved our lives but not by design. We got lucky. Rory won't be so lucky.'

With Bill setting off down the trail and Clifford following on behind, Nat hunched his shoulders and trudged for ten paces.

'But,' Nat said, 'we still got three hundred dollars out of it.'

Clifford laughed and spat on the ground.

'That was *my* three hundred dollars in the

first place.'

'Even so, Rory didn't have to return it to you.'

Clifford shook his head. To block out the low sun he cocked his hat, and then placed a hand on Nat's shoulder.

'He did. That money was the only remaining proof that he accepted my bribe. Rory figured that when we return to Beaver Ridge we might tell the authorities that he released Spenser O'Connor. They'd arrest us but it'd be worth it to ensure that Rory doesn't profit from stealing Kirk. By returning the three hundred dollars he's saying that he's removed the evidence of what happened.'

Nat nodded. 'Except for Spenser O'Connor.'

'Yeah, but he'll be long gone.'

Nat held his hand to his brow and peered into the distance. Only barren rock was ahead.

'How far do you reckon it is to Dust Creek?'

Clifford sighed and held his hand to his brow too.

'At least two days.'

Nat sighed. 'I hope you're wrong.'

Clifford wasn't wrong.

Long into the third day, they staggered to the edge of Dust Creek, a small huddle of buildings hidden in a swirling cloud of dust, their feet blistered and the combination of thirst and hunger bowing their heads.

When they tottered down Dust Creek's only road, Clifford slapped Nat in the stomach.

'We're lucky,' he said, his voice grating.

'Yeah,' Nat muttered, seeing a full horse-trough beside a battered stable. He licked his lips.

'Not the water,' Clifford said, pointing.

Nat turned. Their horses stood outside a store.

'We ain't that lucky,' Nat whispered, 'surely.'

Clifford glanced up and down the road. Only a few other horses were around and none of them belonged to Rory or Spenser.

'Nope. We probably ain't that lucky, but I'll take what I can find.' Clifford hitched his jacket closed and strode to the store, Nat and Bill following. He slammed back the door and they stood in the doorway, enjoying their respite from the hot sun. Then they stormed inside.

The storekeeper trotted from his back store and grinned.

'What can I do for you three gentlemen?'

Clifford cleared his throat and produced a small smile.

'Looking for the man who owns those fine horses outside.'

The storekeeper puffed his chest. 'That'll be me.'

Clifford glanced at Bill and Nat and widened his smile.

'I'd hoped you'd say that. We'd like to buy...' Clifford's voice caught on the word 'buy', and he coughed. 'Yes, buy them off you.'

The storekeeper produced a cloth and

wiped his counter.

'They ain't for sale. They're mighty fine horses, so unless you got more business I got plenty to do.'

'I can tell they're fine horses,' Clifford muttered as the storekeeper turned. 'That's why I want to buy them. But as you're a storekeeper, for you everything has a price.'

The storekeeper turned back and rubbed his chin, appraising Nat and Clifford's obvious footsore state. He gulped when he saw Bill.

'Two hundred dollars is a fair price.'

Clifford winced and then smiled again.

'Might be, but you paid less than that.'

'What makes you think that?'

Clifford slammed both hands on the counter.

'I reckon a group of men rode through here three days ago and they had spare horses.'

The storekeeper shrugged. 'Then you'd be wrong.'

Clifford scratched his head and then nodded.

'In that case a scrawny runt came through Dust Creek three days ago and sold them to you. He was in a hurry and desperate to raise funds and you could tell that. Reckon as you struck a good bargain with him, as you're trying to do with me.'

The storekeeper sighed. 'You know this scrawny runt?'

'Yup. I also know he stole the horses.' Clifford grinned, letting the storekeeper guess the rest.

'In the circumstances I reckon one hundred dollars is a fair price.'

'You'd think so.' Clifford leaned further down on the counter, a long creak emerging from the wood. He grabbed the storekeeper's collar, dragging him over the counter. 'But you can do better than that.'

'Seventy-five,' the storekeeper said with a gulp. 'I paid good money for them.'

'I don't care what you paid,' Clifford said, widening his eyes to glare at the storekeeper. 'Fifty dollars is what I'm offering.'

'I ain't getting out of pocket for this. I paid

in good faith.'

'All right.' Clifford grinned. 'My offer is forty dollars. Better take that before it becomes thirty dollars.'

Clifford slipped his free hand down to his gunbelt and provided his most pleasant smile.

'I paid fifty dollars for those horses and I've fed and watered them. You match that or you'll leave as you arrived – on foot.'

'Thirty dollars.'

The storekeeper narrowed his eyes and glanced to the side.

Nat tensed, reckoning he heard a noise in the back store. He glanced at Clifford, who nodded.

'Thirty dollars is my final offer.' Clifford released his grip a little. 'Plus twenty dollars for information.'

The storekeeper nodded. 'That might be fair.'

Clifford threw the storekeeper back behind his counter and counted out fifty dollars.

The storekeeper straightened his collar and slammed a hand on the notes.

'Nice doing business with you. The man you want headed east and he *was* desperate. Can't say more than that, but that horde of riders you were talking about hurtled through here before him and I reckon he was following them, if that helps.'

'Oh,' Clifford said, glancing at Bill and Nat, 'it helps all right.' Clifford tipped his hat and sauntered outside. He glanced at the saloon next door. Then with a shrug, he mounted his horse and rode it to the trough, where they filled their canteens and gulped down a good share of water.

'You ain't as surprised as I thought you'd be,' Nat said when he'd had his fill.

'You mean about Spenser heading after Kirk?' Clifford said, wiping his mouth with the back of his hand.

'Yeah.'

'I know his type. If Spenser had an ounce of sense, he'd head west, searching for a place where nobody knew him. He has no sense, so he'll head east on who knows what hopeless mission and get himself killed.'

Nat stood straight and sighed. 'We ain't letting Spenser get away with what he did to us either, are we?'

Clifford shook his head. 'If you want to be a bounty hunter, stop thinking that way. Spenser O'Connor is down our list of targets. First we get Kirk Morton back. Second we ensure Rory Johnson suffers for double-crossing us. Guess in doing those we'll get Spenser too, but if not, he'll be next in line.'

11

For three days the group followed the trail east, pushing their horses as much as they dared and cutting down their rest to four hours of sleep and short breaks during the day.

Sufficient recent hoof prints suggested that Rory and his troop of men had passed this way, taking the least populated route to Beaver Ridge.

They also found the remnants of campfires for a group of men and each time they found one, the signs were more recent.

On the morning of the fifth day of pursuit they crested a hill, and further down the hill there was a long line of horses.

Clifford sighed and pulled them from the crest of the hill.

'Now,' he said, 'we stay out of sight and pick our moment.'

They edged from the trail and rode parallel to it, hurrying until they were two miles ahead of Rory. At a narrow gully they stopped and waited, peering down at Rory's line of men as they passed, whispering plans for an ambush, but seeing no obvious way to use their advantage. Rory had twelve men. Six guards flanked Kirk at all times. The remaining guards spread out at the front and back and glared at every passing rock and tree as if an attack was imminent.

Twice more Clifford's group found perfect spots. From good hidden positions they looked down on Rory's men, but each time they saw no way to mount a successful ambush.

So they waited for evening.

When Rory camped down on the edge of a small wood, they tethered their horses in the wood and crept as close to the campsite as possible, hiding on a small mound overlooking it.

They waited for darkness, watching the group's routine and waiting for when they were at their most vulnerable.

In Nat's view, Rory organized his men well. He posted guards at regular intervals on all approaches to the camp-fire, each man slipping down behind bushes or rocks to disappear from sight in the gloom.

In the campsite itself, Rory had six men around Kirk at all times while he allowed the remainder to sleep.

After two hours of watching for mistakes,

Nat slipped along the mound to Clifford.

'This won't be easy,' Nat said.

'Never said it would.'

'But he's doing everything right.'

'Yeah, but we wait until he doesn't. It's a week to Beaver Ridge and he has to do everything right all the time. As soon as he makes a mistake, we'll be waiting for it.'

Nat nodded and then narrowed his eyes. Something moved down the trail. To avoid the moonlight he placed a hand to his brow.

'What's that?' he said.

Clifford stared in the direction Nat looked. He sighed.

'You mean, who's that?'

Nat nodded and leaned on the boulder before him.

A lone rider was galloping along the trail and even in the poor light and from two hundred yards away, the hunched posture suggested this was Spenser O'Connor.

The rider pulled up on the trail level with the campsite and turned. Then, with a huge swipe of his hat against his horse's rump, he hurtled for the campsite.

'What's the damn fool doing?' Nat muttered.

'Getting himself killed I hope,' Clifford said, gesturing along the mound to Bill, who nodded back. 'Watch out for our chance. This'll be a better diversion than we could arrange.'

Spenser hurtled across the ground. At a hundred yards from the campsite, the first gunshot echoed from the guards who'd hidden themselves in the undergrowth. Spenser hunched down further and spurred his horse to greater speed.

Nat glanced at the campsite.

Rory's men rolled from their blankets and barked orders to each other as they organized themselves.

Nat scratched his head. 'I don't know what plan Spenser is trying.'

'Me neither,' Clifford muttered, 'unless he's planning on getting himself killed. That'll work out fine.'

Spenser hurtled into the campsite. He

must have sneaked up on the campsite earlier because he headed straight for the group of men guarding Kirk. Leaning down over the side of his horse, he fired down at the guards, catching two in his wild slew of bullets.

Seeing this was his chance, Kirk head-butted the nearest guard and kicked and struggled from the remainder.

Spenser swung his horse round and reached down.

With his hands tied to his sides, Kirk hopped on the spot, trying to leap on the back of Spenser's horse with ungainly bounds. Spenser grabbed Kirk's shoulders and he rolled over the back of the horse. He was squirming round to sit when Rory's men organized themselves and charged Spenser's horse.

Under excessive gunfire the horse panicked and bolted. As the horse passed, one of Rory's men grabbed Kirk's legs and yanked him from the horse.

Kirk collapsed in a huge cloud of dust,

and three of Rory's men leapt on him, pinning him to the ground.

Spenser surged from the campsite, heading for Rory's horses. With a deft movement, he unhooked a horse from the group and charged back into the campsite, the horse trailing behind.

Up on the mound, Clifford shook his head.

'If he'd arrived with a spare horse, his raid might have worked.'

'You sound like you want him to succeed,' Nat muttered, glaring at Clifford, but Clifford stared down at the campsite.

As Spenser galloped into the campsite, Kirk struggled out from under his tangle of guards. He thrust up his unbound arm, and a glint from the knife Spenser must have passed him shone, as he slashed it across one of the guards.

The other guards fell back, as Kirk scythed the knife across their necks.

Then Kirk charged from the group to the spare horse. This time, he leapt on the horse in a smooth motion. In a huge cloud of dust, he clattered from the campsite, Spenser at his side.

Some of Rory's men dashed after them and laid down a sprinkling of gunfire at their departing forms, all of it wild.

On the mound, Nat glanced to his side.

Clifford had his rifle raised and pointing at Rory's men.

With a lunge, Nat grabbed the rifle barrel, pushing it into the dirt.

'What you doing?' Clifford muttered.

'You were about to fire at Rory's men.'

'And?

'We can take Kirk from Rory but we ain't stopping Rory from recapturing Kirk.'

Clifford snarled and leapt to his feet. Then he cocked his head and dropped on to his front beside Nat. He pointed.

A group of riders emerged from the undergrowth and faced off against the fleeing Spenser and Kirk. They charged forward, corralling the escapees and herding them back.

Spenser fired at them, knocking two men off their horses, and Kirk hurled his knife with deadly accuracy into one man's chest, but the other riders kept coming.

'Who are they?' Nat muttered.

Clifford shrugged.

The riders charged on, bundling around Kirk's horse, cutting off his escape routes. As they bustled, a small gap between two horses appeared, and Kirk galloped through it. But one rider lassoed Kirk around the chest and dragged him off his horse.

Clifford sighed. 'I'll give Spenser this – that plan almost worked.'

'Mad plans often do.'

All the riders grouped around Kirk ignoring Spenser, who wavered a moment, clearly judging his chances. Then, with a huge swipe of his hat against his horse, Spenser spurred it to charge from the campsite, disappearing within seconds into the murk.

With Kirk secure, the riders chortled and waved their hats above their heads as they trotted to the campsite.

Kirk trundled along behind, trying to stagger to his feet. He failed and let the riders drag him into the campsite.

Once Kirk was back, several men surrounded his prone body and lined up to kick him in the guts. Then they bundled him into the centre of the campsite and tied him to a tree stump.

A file of five men jumped on their horses and gesticulated down to Rory, who gestured up at them, his barked orders almost carrying to Nat and Clifford's position.

'Go on,' Clifford muttered. 'Chase after Spenser. He's taken a few of your men so go after him.'

'Yeah,' Nat said. 'If they chase him, we might have a chance.'

Then, with an angry swipe of his arm, Rory pointed to the ground and the men dismounted.

'Damn Rory's sensible hide,' Clifford muttered. When the men were on the ground, they spread out around the campsite's perimeter and knelt. With their guns facing outwards, they prepared for further attacks.

Nat pushed back from his intense watching of Spenser's ambush. 'Guessing as we ain't attacking.'

'Nope,' Clifford said with a sigh. 'For the rest of the night they'll be ready for anything. But we'll have other nights.'

'So who were those other men?'

'Other friends of Rory's. Except we didn't see them. It's a good idea to have an alternative plan.'

Nat noted the admiration in Clifford's voice.

'Yeah. Pity we ain't got one.

Clifford stood and slipped back from their lookout position. Nat followed him and they collected Bill, but once they were out of sight of the campsite Clifford mounted his horse.

'Where you heading?' Bill asked.

'Rory ain't mad enough at Spenser to go

after him.' Clifford grinned. 'But I am.'

Without waiting for a retort, Clifford swung his horse around and headed in a long arc back into the hills, leaving Bill and Nat shrugging at each other.

Clifford charged down to the approach to the campsite following Spenser's obvious trail through the grass. He kept his pace under control as he prepared for a long chase. He galloped for a mile.

Then Spenser appeared ahead, his shape distinct in the moonlight, arcing towards the main trail.

Clifford grinned and slowed, saving his horse for the main chase. He followed for a further mile. Then Spenser reached the trail and Clifford spurred his horse to extra speed.

Ahead Spenser hurtled down the trail, straining his horse to the utmost. He glanced over his shoulder and swirled back to lean further over his horse.

With each long stride, Clifford gained on Spenser.

Every few dozen strides, Spenser glanced over his shoulder.

Using a last burst of speed, Clifford drew alongside. Spenser glanced to his side. With a short lunge, he thrust the reins into one hand and reached back to his holster.

In an instant decision, Clifford swung his horse in towards Spenser. He lifted in the saddle and leapt across the gap between the two horses. He hit Spenser a glancing blow across the shoulders and, with a great clawing lunge, pulled him over the side of his horse. In a huge cloud of dust, they hit the ground and rolled to a long scraping standstill.

Clifford staggered to his feet and rubbed a hand across his chest in bemusement that he hadn't broken anything from his sudden mad action. Then he glanced around, finding that Spenser lay ten feet from him. He stalked to him and hauled him to his feet.

With his eyes rolling, Spenser glared up at Clifford. 'You could have killed both of us,' he muttered.

'Yeah,' Clifford said and clubbed Spenser across the jaw. 'Reckon as it'd have been worth it.'

As Spenser lay on the ground, rubbing his head, Clifford pulled his gun and aimed it down at Spenser.

'Go on,' Spenser muttered. 'Get it over with.'

'You ain't getting away with it that easy.' Clifford wrapped a large hand around Spenser's collar. 'You're coming with me.'

12

'You reckon they're staying in there?' Nat asked.

Clifford sighed. After Spenser's failed attempt to free Kirk last night they'd tracked Rory's troop of men through a long morning. In mid-afternoon Rory had ridden into the small town of Harmony, hidden deep in the hills.

Clifford had directed his group through the trees and around Harmony. In a hidden spot back from the trail to Beaver Ridge, they'd waited for an hour for Rory to emerge.

Bill sighed. 'Reckon as they're enjoying the saloon.'

'Nope,' Nat said. 'Spenser's panicked them. Rory is probably hiring reinforcements to ensure he gets Kirk to Beaver Ridge.'

Clifford rubbed his chin and grinned.

'Yeah,' Clifford said. 'But anything Rory can do, I can do too. Except the kind of men I'll hire ain't the sort Rory would hire and they'll understand how to win this fight.'

For another hour they waited, back from the trail, but Rory's men stayed in Harmony and, as the sun edged towards the hills, the waiting preyed on their nerves.

Nat sighed. 'Rory didn't deal with Bill. Perhaps he ought to head into Harmony and see what's happening.'

Bill nodded. 'Yeah. Why not? It's better than hanging around.' Clifford shrugged and Bill trotted into Harmony. Forty minutes later he emerged, his scarred chin set firm.

'Go on,' Clifford muttered. 'Give me the worst.'

'Rory ain't leaving Harmony. He's pulled up outside a store and he and his men are sitting around in there.'

'That's good news. It gives us plenty of time to plan an attack.'

'Yeah, but a small sheriff's office is in Harmony too and I reckon it has a cell. Rory's handed over Kirk to Sheriff Simmons.' Bill sighed. 'We've lost this battle before we've started.'

Nat and Clifford left Bill guarding Spenser and rode into Harmony.

The town had less than a dozen buildings on either side of a short road and aside from the sheriff's office, it contained a store and a saloon. This high into the hills, the town received few visitors and the run-down buildings reflected the minimal interest the townsfolk had in attracting more people to stop, but the views of the surrounding hills and trees more than made up for the lacklustre town.

'What can we do?' Nat asked when they'd hitched their horses outside the saloon. 'Maybe Bill is right. We've lost this fight if Rory's handed over Kirk to the law.'

'Got no choice but to check out the details,' Clifford said. 'I'll speak to Sheriff Simmons.'

'Want help?'

Clifford shook his head. He stalked across the road and swaggered to a halt, facing the sheriff's office.

'Sheriff Simmons,' he shouted, holding his hands around his mouth. 'Would like a word with you.'

Clifford waited, tapping his boot.

Rory Johnson slipped through the door, smiling.

Clifford gritted his teeth and glanced away while he took deep breaths.

'Howdy, Clifford.' Rory shouted, his voice high and amused. 'You heading to Beaver Ridge too?'

'Sure am,' Clifford muttered.

'You enjoy your walk to Dust Creek?'

Clifford kicked at a stone and spat on the ground. 'It was fine.'

'You stopping here long? Because I reckon you owe me a drink for saving your life.'

'I ain't stopping.'

'Then what are you waiting for?'

'I'm waiting for my prisoner to leave with me.'

Rory shrugged. 'And what prisoner would that be?'

Clifford took a deep breath. 'Kirk Morton.'

'That's strange. I reckon Kirk is my prisoner.'

'He's mine,' Clifford said, spitting each word, 'and he's coming with me.'

'That'd be wrong on both counts.'

Clifford glared at Rory, slamming his fist

against his thigh. Then he backed a pace.

'Ain't here to argue with the likes of you. I want to talk to Sheriff Simmons.'

Rory shrugged. 'The sheriff don't want to talk to the likes of you.'

'Get him out here,' Clifford muttered, enunciating each word.

'As you asked so nicely.'

Rory grinned and sauntered back to the office. He stopped in the doorway and glanced up and down the road. He lifted a foot and rested it across his knee, staring at his boot a moment. With steady care, he picked a piece of dirt from his boot and inspected it.

'Just get him out here,' Clifford roared.

Rory shrugged. 'Did you enjoy watching us foil Spenser's rescue attempt last night? You deserved some entertainment for your time spent watching us. You really are bad at spotting people following you. My other group followed you all day without you noticing.'

Clifford gripped his hands into tight fists

and kicked at the ground, sending a large flurry of dirt into the air.

'Stop winding me up or … or...'

'Or what?' Rory said as he turned.

Clifford snarled and with a wide smile, Rory sauntered into the office. Clifford stood for long minutes, the hot sun blasting on his back, until the sheriff strode from the office.

'Heard you want to see me,' the sheriff said.

'Sure do,' Clifford roared and then gritted his teeth. He continued in a softer voice. 'If you don't mind.'

The sheriff nodded and strode from his office. He was a rangy man, hard-boned and grizzled, typical of lawmen in frontier towns. He stood before Clifford with his hands on his hips and tipped back his hat.

'Ain't sure I want to hear what you're about to say.'

Clifford snorted. 'I'm still saying it. Rory Johnson stole my prisoner and I'm here to reclaim him.'

'You mean Kirk Morton?'

'Who else would I mean?' Clifford shouted, spit spurting from his mouth.

The sheriff backed a pace. 'Ain't responding well to you shouting at me.'

Clifford took a deep breath. 'Look. This is rough on me. I've spent some time searching for Kirk Morton. Then I found him. I risked everything to capture him and then Rory Johnson steals him for the bounty.'

The sheriff laughed and ran a hand over his bristled cheeks.

'And you arrested Kirk out of a pure desire to do good for the state I suppose?'

'You know why we do what we do.'

'Sure, and I ain't caring who is in the right here.' With a sinking pain in his gut, Clifford shook his head.

'Except you're helping Rory keep Kirk.'

'I ain't,' the sheriff said with a shake of his head. 'Rory delivered Kirk into my custody and I've arrested him. Rory is helping me until I can hand over Kirk to the authorities. They'll know the full extent of his crimes.'

'Still sounds to me that you've sided with Rory's story.'

'I ain't caring about Rory's story. The only thing I care about is that Kirk Morton is behind bars. When Marshal Peters arrives, I'll hand over Kirk and that's the end of it.'

Clifford stared down the road, flexing and unflexing his hands. 'When's Marshal Peters coming?'

'That information is private, but when he does, I'll ensure he listens to your story and Rory's story and he can decide who has the best claim on Kirk. Either way, he'll agree with me that the most important thing is to keep Kirk in custody. Sorting who gets the bounty ain't as important.'

'It is to me.'

'Is that a threat?'

Clifford sighed. 'I got no reason to threaten the law.'

'Glad to hear it.' The sheriff nodded and walked round to stand beside Clifford. Staring back at his office, he shrugged and smiled. 'Come on, Clifford. I understand your problem, but Kirk Morton is staying in my cell until the marshal arrives and then it's up to you to talk to him. In the meantime, I want no trouble. Have we got an understanding?'

Clifford sneered and stalked back across the road, leaving the sheriff in the middle of the road shaking his head. Without a word, Clifford stormed by Nat and back to his horse.

With a glance at the sheriff, Nat chased after him.

'I heard some of that,' Nat shouted.

'Yeah and that Rory has wound me up too far. Just because I didn't know his men were tracking us, don't mean I...' Clifford trailed off and waved an arm.

'If it helps, I didn't spot anybody following us either. They knew what they were doing.'

'Yeah, it helps.'

'And we also have a good case to put to the marshal.'

Clifford swirled round and shook his fist.

'You reckon that do you?'

'Yeah,' Nat said, tipping back his hat. 'We won't get the whole bounty, but if the marshal is fairminded, he'll see that we were part of the group that took Kirk. We'll get something.'

Clifford sighed and shook his head.

'Fine theory my young friend.' Clifford glanced at the sheriff's office where the sheriff threw closed his door. 'But you see, Marshal Peters and me have met before and he won't side with me.'

Night had arrived when they returned to the campsite, a chill descending quickly in the hills.

Clifford leapt down from his horse and warmed his hands by the fire that Bill had lit.

Nat waited until Clifford had stared at the flames for a few minutes, then he hunkered down beside him.

'When did you meet Marshal Peters?'

Clifford sighed. 'It's a long story, but we had a dispute over a prisoner. To cut the story short – he hates my methods. The story he'll believe ain't mine.'

Nat nodded. 'Perhaps it's time to give up.'

'We ain't,' Clifford shouted and threw a stray twig into the fire.

'We could. Carrying on is asking for trouble we don't need.'

'We can't stop. I've put good time into tracking Kirk Morton. I deserve that bounty and no two-bit lawman and lousy jailer is coming between me and that six thousand dollars.'

Bill snorted. 'And no two-bit lawman and lousy jailer is coming between me and my revenge.'

'I know,' Nat said, shaking his head, 'but we're alive and we're not down on the deal.'

Bill turned his back and Clifford spat into the fire, the fire sizzling.

'How do you figure that?'

'Rory returned the three hundred dollars.'

'He did at that.' Clifford rubbed his chin. A slow grin spread across his face and he stood. 'Thanks for the idea.'

'What idea?'

Clifford continued grinning. He stalked to Spenser, who sat rubbing his sore spots.

'What do you want?' Spenser muttered.

'I got me an idea.'

Spenser rubbed his elbow, keeping his gaze down. 'Why do I reckon I won't like that idea?'

Clifford stood over Spenser and whistled through his teeth. 'Because you ain't as stupid as you look. I reckon a minor outlaw like you can help us.'

'That ain't likely to happen.'

'The only reason you is still alive is I reckoned you could help us get Kirk. And I've worked out how you can do that.'

Spenser rolled to his feet and stood before Clifford. As he had to look up at Clifford, he turned and strode back five paces.

'I won't help you get Kirk out of Harmony's jail. Unless you ain't worked it out yet, I never intended to help you capture Kirk. I did whatever I needed to do to survive, but I planned to help Kirk avoid your clutches.'

'I never doubted that,' Clifford said, grinning. 'So I have no problem with you.'

'Then what are you saying?'

'I'm saying that you can help me get Kirk out of the sheriff's office and back in my tender care. When I have him, you and I part company. Then you can try and get Kirk back from me. You'll fail but that ain't important right now.'

'I'd sooner die.'

'You've got another dead man's choice. Except this time you'll die in ten seconds if you don't do what I want.' Clifford shrugged. 'So do we have a deal?'

Spenser stared at Clifford, lasting the moment long past his allotted time.

'Depends what the plan is.'

'We go into Harmony. Then Nat–'

Nat jumped to his feet and stormed across the campsite to Clifford. 'You're stopping your plans right there.'

Clifford glared at him. 'Why?'

'Because this is where you and I part company.'

'We had a deal. You said you're a man who never goes back on his word.'

Nat nodded. 'And I am. My deal with you was to capture Kirk and share the bounty in equal portions.'

'That's still the deal.'

'Except I went along with that because I wanted to be a different kind of lawman – the kind that earns enough to make the risks worthwhile. Even so, I still wanted Kirk behind bars. Your plan to capture him from Rory and Sheriff Simmons might give him a chance to escape.'

Clifford laughed. He glanced at Spenser and laughed some more.

'Nope. Spenser ain't got a hope of freeing Kirk. So we still have our deal.'

'Except Spenser will agree with your plans because he reckons Kirk has a chance of escape. I ain't wanting that. Kirk should stay arrested. I'd like to collect on him, but if that ain't happening, I'm still glad he's behind bars. Whatever your problems with Marshal Peters, we should wait for him.'

'And what about my revenge?' Bill asked.

'Revenge never helped any man. Kirk will get what he deserves.'

Bill glared at the fire and, with his hands on his hips, Clifford shook his head.

'You *are* a strange man,' Clifford muttered. 'You're that type of lawman I didn't think existed. The type that never takes a bribe, always raises their hats to womenfolk, always–'

'Quit trying to insult me,' Nat said. He lifted his hat and batted away dust against his thigh. Then he turned and strode towards his horse. 'I ain't a lawman any more, but I have principles and you've crossed them. I'll say goodbye, unless you try to get Kirk out of jail, then I'll be seeing you sooner.'

'Stop!' Clifford roared.

Nat walked another pace and then stopped and turned.

'Say it and then I'm leaving.'

'I want you to answer me one question.' Clifford spat on the ground. 'Why has

Sheriff Simmons allowed Rory Johnson to stay in Harmony?'

'Because Rory brought him in.'

'Nope.' Clifford licked his lips. 'It's because Rory has offered him a slice of the bounty.'

With his eyes narrowed, Nat shook his head.

'You can't know that.'

'I know how things work in the frontier towns, far from the safe world you once worked in.'

Nat shrugged. 'That changes nothing. If the situation were reversed, you'd offer the sheriff an incentive too, and even if the sheriff has taken a cut, Kirk is behind his cell bars and that's where he should stay until Marshal Peters arrives.'

'And what happens then?'

Nat waved a hand at Clifford and turned.

'I ain't debating this with you. Nothing you can say can make me stay.'

'Fine. Go,' Clifford shouted at Nat's back. 'But don't think your ex-fellow lawmen are honest men. Do you want to know why Marshal Peters didn't side with me before?'

Nat sighed. He stopped with his foot raised beside his horse and shook his head.

'Go on,' he said, lowering his foot. 'I got time to hear this.'

Clifford glanced at Spenser and then sauntered to Nat's side.

'We argued over who captured an outlaw,' he said, with his voice low. 'He won and took him in.'

Nat turned and stared at Clifford, shaking his head.

'You telling me that Marshal Peters claimed on the bounty that was yours?' he whispered, guessing that Clifford didn't want Spenser to hear this.

'Nope. It's worse. I'm telling you that the outlaw never reached jail. He bought his freedom.'

'Never,' Nat whispered, his stomach grumbling at the thought.

'Yup. The outlaw spent his time with me talking up the price for letting him escape, except I got enough principles not to take his bribe.'

'You ain't got principles.'

Clifford smiled, adding a nod to Nat's incredulous stare.

'Marshal Peters ain't got the few principles I've got. He took the outlaw off my hands and later I learnt he'd escaped.'

'But you have no proof?'

'Nope. Wouldn't do any good if I did, but the way I see it, we all have the same plans. We want Kirk captured. Taking him in to Beaver Ridge ourselves is the only way we can ensure he stays captured.'

'You saying Marshal Peters will take on all of Rory's men?'

'Yeah. If the price is high enough.'

Nat glanced around the camp-fire, but with nobody else to put his trust in, he sighed.

'How can I believe you?'

'You can't, but from what you've seen of our lawmen out here and the jailers who run our jails, do you reckon what I've said might be true?'

Nat stared at the ground, sighing. 'All right. I'll believe you and even if you're lying, taking matters into our own hands sounds a good idea.'

'So, Spenser,' Clifford said, turning and raising his voice. 'As Nat is still with this happy band, are you?'

Spenser looked up and shrugged. 'Like I said. It depends on whether I like the sound of your plan.'

Clifford stalked round the camp-fire, his lips pursed against a wide grin that threatened to break out.

'You won't like it. You see for starters, you're facing the noose again.'

13

Two hours into the cold spring morning the group rode towards Harmony from their campsite.

Nat slipped his horse closer to Clifford.

'I ain't liking your plan. There has to be a better way.'

'I'm open to ideas. You have two minutes before we reach Harmony.'

Nat glanced ahead at Bill and Spenser.

'It's Spenser that's worrying me. He's only helping us because he wants to free Kirk. That'll end badly. We should do this on our own.'

'Forget Spenser,' Clifford said, lowering his voice. 'He'll fail. If you're happy to face Kirk Morton, Spenser is nothing.'

'I know. You keep saying.'

Clifford drew his horse closer to Nat and

slowed. He waited until the lead horses were a dozen yards ahead.

'Didn't want to say so before,' Clifford said, 'but I talked with Bill earlier. We've changed our plans. Thought I'd save telling you about that until you wavered.'

Nat winced. 'Go on.'

'We intended to take Kirk alive, but hand him in dead. But now Kirk is dying in this raid. Then whether we capture him or fail to ride out of Harmony with him, he won't be enjoying life with all those bullets in him.'

With a steady hand, Nat wiped his forehead, wondering how this fitted in with his old lawman principles. He shrugged.

'Agree with that, but Spenser's only helping us to free Kirk. You promised him that if he goes along with your plans, you'd speak up for him. He won't react well to you double-crossing him.'

Clifford laughed so loud Bill and Spenser turned. He reduced the laugh to a chuckle and they faced the front again.

'It ain't a problem when the likes of

Spenser O'Connor are getting double-crossed.'

Nat sighed. 'This just gets better.'

Nat and the rest of the group pulled up on the edge of Harmony. They sauntered down the short road, Spenser walking ahead of them.

To a nod from Clifford, Nat and Bill hung back and wandered to the saloon opposite the sheriff's office.

Clifford slammed a hand on Spenser's shoulder stopping him ten yards from the office.

'Do what we agreed,' he whispered.

Spenser nodded. 'I know. Except our partnership is about to end and we're on our own.'

'What partnership?' Clifford muttered with a snort and then sighed. 'Yeah, I understand.'

Clifford turned from Spenser and cleared his throat.

'Sheriff Simmons,' Clifford shouted. 'I want to see you.'

He tapped his foot for a minute. Then the

sheriff sauntered outside.

'Thought you wouldn't give up,' the sheriff said, 'so I'll tell you again.'

Clifford lifted his hand from Spenser's shoulder.

'I know. I ain't got a problem with waiting for Marshal Peters. He'll understand the situation when he hears the truth. But I have someonc else to add to your outlaw collection.' Clifford kicked Spenser forward and grinned. 'Except I'd like you to witness that I brought in this one on my own, in case there's bounty.'

The sheriff looked Spenser up and down. He shrugged.

'Who is he?'

Clifford matched the shrug. 'Don't know. He ain't talkative, but he was tracking Rory's group and he raided them, killing some of his men. He's probably a straggler from Kirk Morton's outlaw gang.'

'All right,' the sheriff said. 'I'm much obliged.'

With the side of his boot, Clifford kicked

Spenser forward.

Spenser stumbled, landing face down in the dirt. He rolled to his feet, glaring at Clifford.

'Watch out for him,' Clifford said. 'He ain't good company. If he causes trouble, give him a good kicking.'

The sheriff tipped his hat. 'I always watch out for them.'

The sheriff grabbed Spenser's arm and dragged him inside the office. Clifford watched the office until the door shut. Then he sauntered round and wandered across the road, smiling.

At the other side of the road, he joined Nat and Bill.

'What now?' Bill asked.

Clifford grinned and lifted his eyebrows.

'We wait for the fun to start.'

Spenser O'Connor sat on the cell floor and looked around the office beyond.

In such a small town, the sheriff's office was only a rough shack. The cell was a small barred area in the corner of the room.

Kirk lay on his bunk staring at the ceiling. Scattered about the office were the sheriff and two deputies he'd rustled up when Kirk had arrived. Several of Rory's men were in the room too, with the rest hanging about in the adjoining store.

'You like what you see?' Kirk Morton said, his voice too low to carry beyond the cell.

Spenser shuffled round to sit beside Kirk. 'I ain't ever taken with sitting in a cell.'

'Don't matter,' Kirk muttered, his voice tired. 'Only thing on my mind is what you did at the hideout.'

Spenser shivered. 'Yeah, but I had no choice with those bounty hunters.'

Kirk swung round to sit on his bunk and peered down at Spenser, his eyes bright.

'You had a choice. You could have led them away.'

'They had me trapped.'

'Then you could have warned me when you reached the hideout.'

Spenser gulped and picked at his sleeve.

'You'd have killed me.'

'And?'

Spenser looked up and shrugged.

'So I intended to shoot them when I'd lured them into your hideout, but that Clifford didn't wait for my signal.'

'So what?' Kirk said, turning to stare around the room. 'All I saw is you running.'

'It ain't that simple, but I tried to rescue you.'

'Yeah, and that's why I ain't killed you yet. As a reward, I'm picking my moment.'

Spenser gulped and pulled at Kirk's arm, dragging him closer.

'You won't need to,' Spenser whispered. 'I'm getting you out.'

Kirk snorted. 'Brave talk.'

Spenser shook his head and shuffled round to sit on the bunk beside Kirk. He glanced around the cell, confirming everybody was ignoring them, and then scratched at his shirt cuff with his fingernail. He rubbed at a bare spot and poked out the end of the wire he'd looped inside the cuff.

With his arm leaned towards Kirk, he gazed outside the cell.

Kirk slipped his hand to Spenser's arm and pulled on the wire, stuffing it under his jacket in a quick move.

'That's all I could smuggle in,' Spenser whispered. 'The sheriff is careful.'

'It'll do.' Kirk widened his eyes. 'Look for our chance and you might yet live.'

'I'll speed up that chance.' Spenser stood and sauntered to the front of the cell. He leaned on the bars and coughed.

The sheriff looked up. 'What?'

'I need to talk.'

'You've only been in there ten minutes.' The sheriff sighed. 'I'll go through it again. There's a bucket in the corner and–'

'I know the score. I need to talk to Rory Johnson.'

The sheriff shrugged and called to Rory, who wandered in from the next-door store.

Rory stopped five yards from the cell. 'What you got to say?'

Spenser glanced around the cell and shook

his head.

'I'd like to speak to you in private.'

'Ain't much privacy in here.'

'Then come closer.' Spenser widened his arms. He gripped the bars and lowered his voice. 'This is for your ears only.'

With a glance at the unheeding sheriff, Rory nodded. He reached down and unhooked his gunbelt. He held it out to one of the men, Tom, and wandered to the cell, standing on the edge of Spenser's potential reach.

'Say what you got to say.'

Spenser glanced at the sheriff and then pressed his face between the bars.

'I recognize you from Beaver Ridge jail. You were one of my jailers and I reckon a couple of the other men in here are from the jail too.'

Rory shrugged. 'So you've got a good memory.'

'I have and I reckon that bounty hunter organized some dubious deals to get me out. I don't know the details of what you and he did, but I've pieced together enough to reckon it's an interesting story.'

'And why would that story interest me?'

Spenser lifted a hand from the bars to rub his chin. He smiled. 'Reckon as it might be something we should discuss. Perhaps we should work out what the full details are.'

Rory waved a hand at him and backed a pace.

'You got nothing to discuss with me. When we return you to Beaver Ridge you'll swing as you nearly did before.'

'Except I've visited the noose,' Spenser whispered, lowering his voice so that Rory paced forward to hear him. 'I've met several people who'd heard I'd died. When we reach Beaver Ridge, you can't hang a dead man.'

Rory stared at him, breathing deeply thorough his nostrils.

'That's a good theory. I'm looking forward to testing it.'

'Except we won't test it. I ain't stupid. I won't live to reach Beaver Ridge. You'll arrange for something to happen to me when I leave this cell.'

Rory chuckled, nodding. 'Then enjoy yourself in that cell. Condemned men get a few days to find peace with their maker. I suggest you do that.'

'I intend to.' Spenser pressed his face through the bars, resting his chin on the horizontal slat. 'But before then, I'll tell my story to the sheriff.'

Rory glanced at the sheriff, who leaned back in his chair, whistling. He edged forward a half-pace and threw out his hands to grip the bars on either side of Spenser's hands.

'You ain't got a story. You know nothing.'

Spenser shrugged and wrapped his hands tight around the bars.

'I know enough to interest a sheriff.'

'That won't help you. You'll still swing if you tell him.'

'I *will* swing,' Spenser said and licked his lips, 'but I won't be the only one who'll swing if I convince him.'

'You said it. *If* you convince him, I might face trouble, but nobody will worry about the likes of you getting conned into helping a bounty hunter or me letting you out of jail.' Rory nodded over Spenser's shoulder at Kirk. 'Not when Kirk Morton is behind bars.'

'I know you've offered the sheriff a cut on Kirk's bounty, and you think you're safe. But I'm betting that won't stop a lawman from arresting you for what you did, however grateful he is for you bringing in Kirk Morton.'

Rory raised his eyebrows. 'I wish you luck.'

'So you don't want to stop me?'

'You've got nothing to gain from this.'

Spenser shrugged and cleared his throat. He stared over Rory's shoulder at the sheriff and then turned to Rory.

'I ain't,' he muttered, 'but you've got more to lose.'

Rory hung his head and kicked his foot against the base of the bars. He sighed.

'Let's hear it. What do you want?'

Spenser bent to look up into Rory's face.

'I want nothing from you. I want what I always wanted. I want to live.'

'Difficult to see how that will help me.'

'Because I'll do the one thing you want. You'll never see me again. Get me out of this cell and I'll leave Harmony so fast you'll see nothing but a trail of dust. Those bounty hunters are hanging around outside so I'll head out the back and take a horse – you've got a few spare – I'll head west and keep on until I've put Kansas behind me. What you did in Beaver Ridge jail will remain hidden for ever.'

Rory lifted a hand from the bars and rubbed his chin. He stared into Spenser's deep-set eyes.

'You won't do that. You ain't to be trusted. You'll try to free Kirk again.'

'Don't push me, Rory.'

'You won't say anything,' Rory said with a steady shake of his head.

'Sheriff,' Spenser shouted, causing Rory to flinch back.

The sheriff looked up and rose from his desk.

'What now?' he said with a yawn.

'I've finished with Rory. I need to talk to you. I have something you'd like to hear.'

The sheriff nodded and sauntered across his office to join Rory. 'I'm listening.'

As Spenser opened his mouth, Rory lifted a hand. 'I'll speak for him,' Rory said.

'This man can speak for himself,' the sheriff said.

'It'll sound better if it comes from me. Me and…' Rory sighed. 'Me and Jed have sorted our differences.'

'Jed,' the sheriff said, 'this man's name is Jed?'

'Yeah. He's Jed Simpson.'

'Never heard of him. What else do you know?'

'He ain't part of Kirk Morton's gang,' Rory said with a shrug. 'He was one of my men.'

'Why didn't you say so?' the sheriff snarled. 'I ain't happy with you messing me around.'

'It was difficult for me.' Rory coughed. 'When I assembled a team I trawled Beaver Ridge's saloons and Jed joined us. You know what a team drawn from the roughest saloons in town is like.'

The sheriff nodded. 'They quarrelled and fought about anything and everything?'

'Yeah,' Rory glanced at Spenser and shook his head. 'Some of my men kicked Jed out of the group after one fight too many. Jed tracked us and squared up to the men that had wronged him. He killed them. In the confusion Kirk tried to escape, but that didn't work.'

'But Jed still killed some of your people?'

'He did.' Rory turned and gestured to Tom. 'Tom, you can confirm that the matter is closed. Jed had good cause to do what he did.'

Tom glared at Rory and then nodded.

'You're right,' Tom said. 'Got no reason to detain Jed.'

The sheriff nodded and glanced into the cell.

Kirk sat at the back staring at the floor and ignoring this conversation.

The sheriff gestured to a deputy, who rummaged in the desk and removed the cell key.

With a smile to Rory, Spenser backed from the cell door. He maintained his smile as the deputy opened the door. Spenser slipped through the door and stood aside as the deputy shut the door and locked it.

'Jed,' the sheriff said. 'You're free to go.'

Spenser glanced at the front door. 'I'll head out the back. I want to avoid that bounty hunter. I don't want trouble from him or anyone.'

'That's a fine desire.'

Spenser tipped his hat to Rory. 'I'll be taking my old horse, where is he?'

Rory took a deep breath. 'He's out back at the end, Jed. I want you to stay away, if I see you again, I–'

'I know,' Spenser said, shaking his head, 'I know.'

Spenser smiled and with a last nod to the

sheriff, he wandered past the cell. He gave the barest nod into the cell to Kirk and then clubbed his left hand in a backhanded blow at the deputy, knocking him against the cell bars. Carrying the motion on, he lunged for the sheriff's holster.

The sheriff slammed his hand on top of Spenser's, but Spenser clubbed him on the jaw with his other hand, felling him.

As Spenser scrambled on the floor for the unconscious sheriff's gun, Kirk leapt to the front of the cell and wrapped an arm through the bars and around the deputy's neck. He slipped the wire from his jacket and pulled it up and around, garrotting the deputy with an angry pull back of his hand. Tom leapt forward trying to save the deputy, but Spenser had the sheriff's gun to hand and shot Tom low to the belly.

Without his gunbelt, Rory backed. He glanced at the cell where Kirk was rummaging the keys from the deputy's belt, and dashed into the store at the side, shouting orders.

The cell door flew open and crashed back against the bars. Kirk dashed out. He grabbed the deputy's gun and grinned up at Spenser. 'Good work,' Kirk said.

'Like I promised. What's the plan?'

'We go out the back.'

Spenser nodded. He waited while Kirk grabbed the second gun from Tom and then charged to the back door.

They stood on either side of the door and Spenser threw it open, but a hail of bullets blasted into the doorframe and he threw it closed. 'They've organized themselves quick.'

Kirk nodded and Spenser slipped to the entrance to the store. The adjoining room was empty.

'Yeah, but we're free of the cell,' Kirk said. 'We have a chance.'

'What we doing, boss?'

Kirk grinned and turned to Spenser, his eyes bright. He glanced at the sheriff and shook his head.

'Pity I ain't got time to cut him up, but we is getting out of here.'

14

As gunshots echoed inside the sheriff's office, Clifford grinned and without a word, Nat and Bill spread out down the road outside the saloon.

Seconds later, Rory and a file of men dashed from the store. Half of the men dashed round the back of the shack, the others spreading out down both sides of the road, taking cover behind barrels and anything they could find.

More gunfire blasted from behind the shack. Nat slipped along the road to Clifford.

'You reckon we should head out the back of the office if they're trying to break out that way?' Nat asked.

'Nope. Kirk Morton is the kind of man who won't sneak out the back. He'll take his chances on this side.'

'Let's hope you're right.'

Clifford cleared his throat.

'Rory Johnson,' he shouted. 'You sound like you're having trouble.'

Rory jumped up from the barrel he was hiding behind and glared down the road at Clifford.

'Should have known that you and Spenser O'Connor cooked up that stupid scheme.'

'Spenser ain't working with me. He's trying to save himself and Kirk.'

'He'll fail.'

'In that you're right, but let's forget our differences and work together.'

Rory shrugged. 'Nope, Clifford. Kirk Morton is my prisoner.'

Clifford laughed. 'To be a bounty hunter, you must capture and keep the outlaw. You ain't done that. The bounty is open again and whoever gets Kirk gets that bounty.'

Rory peered over his barrel at the sheriff's office and then stood with his hands on his hips.

'What you saying, Clifford?'

Clifford stood, but kept his gun arm aimed at the office. 'I say we have one aim here.'

'Yeah. You want me dead, and I ain't got good feelings about you either now.'

'You're right, but we also want Kirk behind bars and we want bounty.'

Rory grinned. 'Except I'm taking it all.'

Clifford nodded towards the office. 'Heard gunfire in there. Reckon as Kirk's killed another lawman. That'll raise his price. When we reach Beaver Ridge, the price on his head will be enough to satisfy both of us.'

Rory spat on the ground. 'All right. Let's hear what you're offering.'

'I'm offering equal shares for you and me. We can spread our share around our men as we see fit.'

Rory waved an arm down the road. 'I got more men than you.'

'Quit quibbling or you'll get nothing.'

Rory rubbed a hand across his brow and sighed.

'Deal.'

Clifford nodded and slipped down beside Nat. With a steady shake of his head, Nat raised his eyebrows.

'Never thought I'd hear you do that. I reckoned you were all for killing Rory before.'

Clifford shrugged. 'Yeah.'

Nat sighed. 'You've got no intention of following through with that promise have you?'

'Quit talking and concentrate. We got a man to take.'

With Clifford turning to glare across the road, Nat slipped down to a comfortable posture with his gun hand rested on top of a barrel.

For a few minutes they waited. Then someone inside the sheriff's office broke the only window and fired outside.

Rory's men ducked behind their cover.

Within seconds the door flew open and Kirk dashed outside and down the road, firing at Rory's men from his twin guns.

As Nat aimed at Kirk, Spenser dashed from the door, also with a gun in each hand and bullets blasting from both guns across the barrels Nat hid behind.

Nat hit the ground, waiting for the barrage to end. As soon as the firing stopped, he nudged his head above the barrel.

Half a dozen bodies lay in the road. Spenser and Kirk had taken cover behind a collection of barrels half-way down the road on the other side.

'This is wrong,' Nat whispered, appraising the remainder of Rory's forces. 'They might escape.'

'They ain't,' Clifford muttered.

'You engineered this situation. You'd better sort it out.'

'I'm open to suggestions.'

Nat gazed along the road. Thirty yards away on his side of the road Rory and several men were hiding behind a log-pile and several more men were at the corner of the sheriff's office. These were the only people left out of Rory's original group.

Barrels and log-piles provided plenty of cover on both sides of the road, but crossing the road to get close to Kirk and Spenser was impossible.

Nat glanced up and smiled. 'Lay down cover. I'm heading across the road.'

'Ain't the right time to do that. They'll pick you off.'

Nat shook his head. 'I ain't planning on dying. I'm taking the long route.'

Clifford raised his eyebrows and then leaned on the barrel before him. With Bill, he blasted at Kirk's position while Nat jumped to his feet and dashed down the road away from them.

Nat ran as fast as he could until he was a hundred yards from the last of Harmony's buildings and then slowed to catch his breath. Then he crossed the trail leading into town and headed in a long arc back to the buildings, keeping the road out of view.

Rory's men, who had positioned themselves at the corner of the sheriff's office, watched him approach.

Nat waved to them and headed around the back of the sheriff's office. Once there, Nat stared at the roof and sighed, not seeing how to get on the roof. Then he saw a water-barrel and rolled it to the wall.

He jumped on the barrel and leapt up, grabbing the edge of the roof. With both elbows, he levered off his feet and swung up on to the boarding.

He lay a moment catching his breath, and then crawled up the roof. The thin wooden slats beneath him creaked and Nat stopped. He edged his hands forward, checking his path up the roof, and restarted his steady journey.

When Nat reached the rooftop, he peered at the road below. Clifford and Bill were crouched down on the other side of the road and Rory's men were hiding further along the road.

When nobody looked at him, Nat sighed in relief, but Clifford waved with both hands, palms facing down the road. Nat nodded and edged along the rooftop for five yards to his right. He stared down at Clifford, who nodded. Nat waved and then edged down the side of the roof.

The roof creaked, a slat breaking beneath him.

Nat lay flat, spreading his weight. When he'd checked that the roof supported him, he crouched and mimed the roof breaking by pressing his hands together and then swinging his arms down.

Clifford nodded, Nat taking that to mean that Kirk and Spenser didn't seem to have heard the noise.

With a sigh, Nat repeated the mime and on the third repeat, with a shared nod, Clifford fired over the barrel at Kirk's position, Bill taking over, while Clifford reloaded.

As they were now covering the noise he was making, Nat snaked down the roof, keeping as low as possible.

Moving with his head facing down, he sidled to the end of the roof, but as he neared the edge, he noted a further problem.

The sun blasted down on his back from a cloudless sky, throwing his shadow into stark relief across the roof. Before he reached the roof edge that shadow would fall on the ground right before Kirk and Spenser.

With luck, they wouldn't see the shadow. But if he were unlucky, they'd pick him off before he jumped.

He snaked as close to the edge as he could, while keeping his shadow on the roof, and took a deep breath.

Unable to plan his leap, he needed to take his chances.

The sustained gunfire from below stopped and taking that as his cue, Nat rolled from the roof.

As Nat fell, he had a fraction of a second to orient, seeing Kirk below him hunched behind a barrel. Then he landed on Kirk's back and the breath blasted from Nat's chest.

Kirk collapsed beneath him, scattering the barrels in all directions. In his stunned state,

Nat saw Spenser beside him and his fall had caught him a glancing blow too. Nat kicked Spenser on the side of his head to bundle him to the ground.

Then Nat lay winded.

Kirk rolled from beneath Nat. Without the time to kill Nat, Kirk clubbed him against the wall, then dashed from the barrels as Rory's men charged across the road towards him.

Five paces into the road Kirk slid to a halt and, with his shoulders hunched, he swung round, blasting a rapid slew of gunfire from his twin guns, the bullets cutting across everyone in an arc.

Clifford and Bill dashed into the road, a bullet catching Bill in the chest, spinning him round. In a desperate leap, Clifford rolled to the side of the road as Kirk dashed towards the saloon, firing as he ran.

Then Kirk leapt behind the barrels Clifford and Nat had hid behind before.

Nat glanced away and took a deep breath.

Five feet from him Spenser lay, rubbing

his head and staring into the road with his eyes glazed. With a small shake of his head, Spenser turned his gun round to aim at Nat.

As he was still too stunned to pull his gun, Nat glared at Spenser and shook his head.

With a returning shake of his head, Spenser holstered his gun.

Nat was about to thank Spenser when Clifford's shadow fell over him. 'Still obliged,' Nat muttered and lay back.

Clifford grinned. Hunched over, he dragged Spenser's gun from its holster and kicked away the second gun.

'You,' Clifford muttered, 'will stay quiet.'

Spenser rolled back, his eyes closing. Clifford glared at Spenser a moment and then clubbed him across the forehead with the stock of his gun.

Nat rubbed at his forehead, freeing the last of his shakiness. 'Guessing as I'm ready,' he said.

Clifford gestured across the road. 'Kirk got Bill and most of Rory's men and he's holed up on the other side.'

'Yeah, I saw that. I ain't that stunned.'

Clifford chuckled. 'Don't suppose you're ready to do that roof trick on the saloon's roof are you?'

Nat rubbed his temples and sighed.

'Nope. We need another plan.' Nat glanced down the road, confirming that most of Rory's men lay dead in the road. 'And the plan will have to come from us.

Clifford nodded. 'You up to getting Kirk?'

'Yup. What you planning?'

'Had enough of hiding from Kirk behind rocks and barrels. It's time to do this the simple way. We split up. You go left and I go right. With Spenser out of action, he can't fire in both directions.'

Nat nodded. 'Sounds good. When we doing this?'

Clifford grinned. 'Now.'

Nat nodded as Clifford dashed from the barrels, charging down the side of the road. Gunfire blasted around him.

Nat leapt to his feet. He charged in the opposite direction. But as no gunfire blasted at him, he slid to a halt and arced across the road heading for Kirk's position, his gun held at arm's length. He couldn't see Kirk but he gritted his teeth and waited until he had a clear shot.

Further down the road, Clifford arced in towards Kirk too. A bullet ripped across his shoulder and he leapt to the ground, rolling over as he landed.

As Clifford fell, Kirk jumped to his feet, his right hand swinging his gun towards Clifford, his left hand swinging towards Nat.

Nat dived to the ground as a bullet whistled by his ear and came up on one knee. He steadied and fired, catching Kirk a glancing blow across the chest.

Kirk staggered back, his arm thrown across his chest, and Clifford's shot from the ground caught him in the leg. Kirk fell to his knees, his arms dangling by his sides.

Nat kept his gun steadied on Kirk.

'Time to give yourself up,' he shouted.

Kirk chuckled. He stared at Clifford and

grinned, forcing his arms to rise.

Clifford rolled to his knees and when Kirk had dragged up both his guns to almost level with his shoulders, he flicked his wrist and put a bullet clean in the middle of Kirk's forehead.

Nat turned and sighed. While shaking his head, he sauntered down the road, holstering his gun. He stood before Clifford.

Clifford glanced at the rip across his shoulder and shrugged.

'One small nick for six thousand dollars ain't much of a price.' Clifford grinned. 'Stop pouting, Nat. I told you Kirk wouldn't leave Harmony.'

With an outstretched hand, Nat tugged Clifford to his feet.

'Guessing as you had no trouble keeping that promise,' Nat said.

'Nope,' Clifford said. He strode down the road and stared down at Bill, shaking his head.

'Sorry you didn't see Kirk die,' Clifford muttered and strode round to kick at Kirk's body, shaking his head. 'But dead he is.'

Nat wandered from body to body, checking each man was dead, but once he'd checked a dozen men, Rory stepped up from behind a barrel at the end of the road and tipped his hat to Nat.

'You're alive,' Nat said.

'Yeah,' Rory said and sauntered down the road. When he reached Kirk, he looked down at him, shaking his head. 'But he ain't.'

'Yeah,' Clifford muttered. 'The rest of your men weren't so lucky.'

'Seems that way.'

'Didn't see you risking much.'

'I was helping.'

Clifford laughed and gestured at the bodies of Rory's men scattered down the road.

'The way I saw it, you hid while everyone else took the risks.'

'I was ready to take on Kirk if your plan failed.'

'The men that take the risks take the bounty.'

‘Didn’t know that’s how bounty hunting worked. We had a deal.’

‘Our deal was to help each other. You did squat.’

Rory shrugged and strode from Kirk’s body. He glanced at Spenser’s unconscious form and sighed.

‘That ain’t right.’

Clifford shook his head and then turned on his hip, his gun swinging towards Rory.

Rory scrambled for his gun, but as he reached it, a bullet ripped into his upper chest. He spun back to land on his side.

With an outstretched hand, Rory inched down to his gun, but a second gunshot blasted into his belly.

Rory twitched and then lay still.

Clifford smiled and glanced at Nat.

‘You didn’t have to do that,’ Nat muttered.

Clifford shrugged. ‘You don’t understand how this works, do you?’

‘I don’t,’ Nat said, straightening his hat. ‘Got a feeling I don’t want to either.’

Nat propped Spenser against the wall and

dragged several bodies to the side of the road. He looked up when the sheriff's office door opened and the sheriff stumbled out.

'You're too late,' Clifford shouted. 'We've had all the fun.'

'Yeah,' the sheriff muttered, rubbing his forehead. 'You got Kirk?'

'Yup, and his accomplice.' Clifford pulled Spenser to his feet and threw him towards the sheriff. 'His hide is worth squat. You can do whatever you want with him.'

15

An hour after killing Kirk Morton, Clifford ensured Kirk's bonds secured him to a horse. Then he attached that horse to his own horse and turned to Nat.

'You ready to go?' he said.

'As soon as we sort out what we're doing with Spenser O'Connor.'

Clifford shrugged. 'Got us some long riding ahead. Ain't seen no hint of other trouble, but after the past surprises I ain't taking chances. We don't collect the bounty until we hand in Kirk's hide to Beaver Ridge jail so we don't need complications like Spenser.'

'You promised to free Spenser. At the least, you ought to speak up for him. That means we either do that here or we take him with us to Beaver Ridge.'

'I ain't doing the latter, and I ain't wasting the breath on speaking up for him now.'

Nat rubbed his forehead. 'But you promised him and he came through on his side of the deal. He helped us.'

'Promises to creatures like Spenser O'Connor mean squat.' Clifford mounted his horse and grabbed the reins in one fist. 'I'm leaving.'

'And I ain't. We made a promise and I don't go back on those.'

'Please yourself. Don't expect me to wait for you.'

Clifford swung his horse around and galloped out of Harmony in a cloud of dust, heading east.

Nat watched Clifford go and when he'd disappeared into the trees, he shook his head and headed to the sheriff's office. He sauntered inside. The sheriff had righted the furniture and sat behind his desk.

In the small cell in the corner of the room, Spenser sat hunched, his hand wrapped around a bullet nick in his upper arm.

'What's wrong?' The sheriff asked. 'I thought you were heading out of Harmony?'

'I am. I had unfinished business to deal with.' Nat nodded to the cell. 'I'm staying to see that he gets the justice he deserves.'

The sheriff grinned. 'You won't be waiting long. I've sent Deputy Claiborne to round up a few men. As soon as he's got them, we'll be giving Jed the justice he deserves.'

'Jed? That ain't his name. He's Spenser O'Connor.'

'Don't care what his name is. You don't need to know a man's name before you hang him.' The sheriff frowned. 'You ain't saying we shouldn't hang him are you?'

Nat sighed and glanced at Spenser, who nodded, a small smile on his face.

'I am saying that.'

'But he killed a man. From what I've seen, he's probably done a whole lot more besides.'

'From what I remember, you hadn't heard of him until Clifford rode into Harmony. You can't make assumptions like that and hang a man. The way I see it, the wrongs done against Spenser make it difficult to hang him. You can't hang a man twice.'

'Hang him twice. What's that supposed to mean?' The sheriff waved a hand. 'Forget it. I ain't interested.'

'Nat,' Spenser shouted from his cell. 'I'm obliged to you for speaking up for me, but I got no desire to spend my life in jail. I've been minutes away from the noose for a while and I'm tired of avoiding it.'

'You heard what the man said,' the sheriff muttered.

Nat shook his head. 'Ain't so sure he should face the noose. Spenser deserves a proper trial and his help in tracking down Kirk, no matter how self-motivated it was, should be taken into consideration. His help should get his sentence reduced to a few years in jail.'

Spenser tipped his hat. 'Even more obliged if you're right.'

'He ain't right,' the sheriff muttered. 'Spenser ain't getting the chance. You see I ain't hanging him for what he did before, just what he's done since he came into my town. One of my deputies is dead. I don't know what version of the law you're supporting, but killing a lawman is a hanging offence as far as I'm concerned.'

Nat sighed. 'Ain't that simple. Bullets were flying in all directions from everyone. It's anybody's guess who killed your deputy. We should wait until Marshal Peters arrives. We'll let him sort out the truth.'

The sheriff scratched the back of his neck and shook his head.

'No need. I know enough of the truth. So unless you want to help me string him up, you'd better head on out of Harmony.'

'Thanks for trying,' Spenser shouted.

Nat stared at the sheriff long and hard. He nodded.

'You're mighty keen to hang this man. Why is that?'

'My deputy is dead and he was a good friend. You can understand that, can't you?'

'I can, but that ain't the reason.'

The sheriff shrugged. 'Just go.'

'I ain't leaving until you tell me how much Clifford has paid you to hang Spenser.'

'Why should he pay me to hang this worthless creature?'

'Because Spenser's the last loose end. He's the proof of what Clifford and Rory did. Once Spenser's dead, nobody will worry about the identity of a lowlife like him and nobody will figure out that another man died in Beaver Ridge jail instead of him.'

'Go. I ain't got time for this.'

Nat shook his head and turned. In a

sudden decision, he turned back, his hand pulling his gun from its holster.

'I *will* be leaving. Except Spenser will be with me.'

The sheriff glared at Nat and then to Nat's directions, he lifted his hands above his head.

Walking sideways, Nat stalked to the side of the cell and lifted the cell key from the sheriff's desk. Then keeping his gun trained on the sheriff he dangled the key beside the cell.

Spenser reached through the bars and took the key. In a quick gesture, he slipped it into the lock and opened the door.

'You're making a big mistake,' the sheriff muttered.

'You're probably right, but I'll ensure Spenser gets the justice he deserves, and he ain't getting it here. He might face the noose, but he'll face it the right way.'

'Stop trying to sound like a lawman. You're a bounty hunter.'

Nat laughed. 'I'm more of a lawman when

I ain't one than you'll ever be.'

'We'll track you down. You won't live to escape from what's coming to you.'

'You can try.'

Nat gestured to the front door and Spenser slipped by him to head for the door.

The door opened and Deputy Claiborne wandered in. He did a double take and swirled his hand down to his holster.

Without a choice, Nat swung his hand up, firing a single shot through the deputy's shoulder.

The deputy turned, falling to the ground outside, the door swinging shut.

From the corner of his eye, Nat saw the sheriff whirl his arm, and Nat pivoted on his heel, firing from three yards away. He aimed for the sheriff's shoulder, but with only a moment to steady his aim, the gunshot blasted low, hitting the sheriff in the chest.

The sheriff rolled over his desk, landing with a dull thud behind it. Spenser dashed round the desk and knelt beside the sheriff. He looked up and shook his head.

Nat gulped and hung his head.

When he looked up, Spenser had wrapped the sheriff's gunbelt around his waist.

'Looks like we is getting out of here.'

Nat nodded and stalked to the door. He peered outside. The deputy lay beside the door, crawling away by throwing out a clawed hand to drag himself on a few inches.

With a last glance at the dead sheriff, Nat marched through the door and glanced up and down the road. Outside, a group of men pressed back against the wall. He glanced down, confirming they were unarmed cowhands. The nearest man lifted his hands.

'We ain't trouble,' he shouted. 'We're no match for you.'

Nat opened his mouth and then shook his head. He dashed forward and knelt beside the wounded deputy, checking that the gunshot wound was minor. The deputy stared up at him, cowering.

'I ain't giving you no more trouble.'

Nat nodded and turned.

'Watch out!' Spenser shouted.

Nat turned on the hip, his gun arcing towards the deputy.

A bullet ripped out and the deputy fell to his side, his head slamming into the dirt. The deputy's gun fell from his hand.

Nat sighed and turned as Spenser holstered his gun.

'Thanks,' Nat said.

Spenser nodded. He strode across the road to a group of Rory's horses and picked one.

When Nat had mounted his horse, they swung round and galloped out of Harmony, throwing up dust in their headlong dash away.

Every hundred yards, Nat and Spenser glanced over their shoulders, but Harmony's townsfolk stayed in Harmony.

A mile from Harmony, they slowed to a canter and Spenser sighed.

'You know what you've done, don't you?' Spenser said.

'Yeah,' Nat muttered.

'I'm in your debt. Just so you know, I ain't giving you trouble.'

'Glad to hear it.'

'Hope you're right and I'll get a fair hearing in Beaver Ridge.'

Nat pulled on the reins. When his horse stopped, he stood across the trail.

Spenser halted too and then trotted to him.

Nat sighed. 'I can't promise you that.'

'You sounded sure in Harmony.'

'That was the lawman version of me speaking.'

'You sound more convincing as a lawman than as a bounty hunter.'

Nat tipped back his hat. 'You might be right.'

'Then why can't you promise me anything? You know how the law works.'

'Thought I did. When I was a deputy I understood the rules, but since I took up with Clifford Trantor I ain't understood anything any more. The men who are after the outlaws are crooked and the outlaws are more crooked, except they have what I thought lawmen had. They stand by their word and are loyal to their friends.'

'Loyalty is all any man needs to get by.' Spenser smiled. 'And being scared of what your friends might do if you don't help them.'

Nat nodded. 'Whatever your reasons, I ain't taking you in. You're free to go like Clifford and me promised you. What you do with that freedom is up to you, but if I hear you've abused it, I'll be the first one that comes looking for you.'

Spenser shrugged. 'But I left you to die at the hideout.'

'Ain't important that you double-crossed us, because I gave my word and I stick by that.'

'Much obliged. Reckon as we're even and that includes Clifford.'

'It does at that.'

'I'm taking the blame for the lawmen's deaths in Harmony.'

Nat shook his head. 'There's no need to.'

'There is. Besides, whatever the truth, everyone will think I did it.'

'They won't. Remember, as far as everyone is concerned, you're dead.'

'Maybe, but when people look at the likes of me, they'll reckon I'm the killer and not a fair-haired young man like you.' Spenser smiled. 'And I won't deny it. I owe you that.'

Nat tipped back his hat. 'Much obliged.'

'Hope you enjoy the bounty.'

'The bounty won't compensate me for what I've lost. Whatever other people believe, I'll know I'm a man who killed a lawman.'

'A corrupt lawman though!'

'That don't matter.'

'Often think money can help a man forget his ills.'

'I used to think that too. Except I've seen the things that people will do for money and I did some of them myself. I don't want to be that kind of man.'

Spenser stared at Nat and rocked his head to one side.

'You mean that you ain't joining Clifford?'

'Nope. Had enough of spending time with Clifford Trantor. He double-crossed you, Rory, and just about everybody he dealt with. I'm sure he'd do the same to me if I rejoined him. That man's worse than the outlaws he tracks down.'

Spenser shook his head. 'A share in six thousands dollars' worth of bounty can do a lot to cheer up a man.'

Nat shrugged, but Spenser was staring over his shoulder. Nat turned and sighed.

Clifford stood a ways back along the trail, hunched over in the saddle.

'I should have known he wouldn't let this pass,' Nat muttered.

Spenser nodded. 'He won't be happy that I'm alive.'

Nat swung round to stand across the trail before Spenser.

'You decided to wait for me then, Clifford,' Nat shouted.

Clifford shrugged. 'Seems that I did. I thought you wouldn't leave here with matters not sorted out.'

'Everything *is* sorted out.'

'Then why is Spenser free?'

'Because the sheriff was planning to hang him.'

Clifford shook his head. 'Why should that concern you?'

'We had a deal in Beaver Ridge to let Spenser go when he'd led us to Kirk Morton. Spenser has fulfilled that deal and I'm ensuring that this ends how it should.'

'As a lawman you should know you're siding with the wrong kind of person, Nat. Spenser's a killer.'

'I ain't a lawman no more, but all any man can rely on in this world is his word. Soon as you give up that, you ain't a man any more.' Nat took a deep breath. 'As regards our deals. I said I'd help you track down Kirk Morton and we've done that, so our partnership is over now.'

'Then I'll give you a new promise. Spenser's staying in Harmony and dying. Either step aside or die with him.'

'Can't do that, Clifford.'

Clifford shrugged. He released his packhorse and pulled on his reins with one hand. His horse reared as he pulled his gun with the other hand.

Nat pulled his gun but with no view of Clifford, he jumped to the ground, Spenser doing the same behind him.

Nat hit the ground, rolled, and halted lying flat with his gun held before him.

With his head held low behind his horse's head, Clifford charged Nat, giving him no target to aim at.

Nat waited until the last possible second, the horse galloping towards him. Then he realized that Clifford didn't intend to shoot him but was aiming to run him down. He rolled to the side, missing the horse's thundering hoofs by scant inches, the blast of air rushing over him. On his back, Nat just had time for a speculative shot, which was wild.

Then Clifford drew his horse to a halt and swung round ready to try and run down Nat again.

Nat rolled to his feet. He wavered a second and then leapt to the side to roll into the bushes. He glanced up.

Spenser had already hidden and Clifford was charging at Nat, but his horse balked at heading into undergrowth and reared.

Seizing his chance, Nat jumped to his feet and fired up at Clifford. Clifford rolled back off his horse, hitting the ground.

To avoid the panicking, riderless horse, Nat jumped to the side and then knelt. With a quick bob of his head, he stared out from his bush, but Clifford had dashed into hiding.

A small dribble of blood on the ground confirmed he'd hit Clifford. Nat ducked, cursing his bad aim.

He slipped down and crawled quickly through the bushes along the trail, then peered out from a different position.

Again he only saw the trail and the thick bushes on either side.

He hunkered down and dashed, doubled over, along the trail. Then he charged into the bushes, the undergrowth ripping across his face.

His wild dash hadn't persuaded Clifford to reveal his position, so Nat knelt and prepared for a long wait.

Cold metal pressed against the back of Nat's neck and he gulped.

The gun barrel pressed harder and a hand wrapped around his mouth.

'Stay still,' Clifford whispered, levering Nat's gun from its holster.

'Go to hell,' Nat whispered behind Clifford's hand.

'Only thing keeping you alive is I don't want Spenser to know where I am.'

As Clifford released his grip around his mouth, Nat spat.

'Spenser's long gone. That was the deal.'

'His horse is still there.'

'There are others in Harmony.'

Clifford chuckled. 'Be quiet.'

'You don't have to kill Spenser,' Nat whispered. 'He's running. Nobody will discover what you did to get him out of jail.'

'First rule of this business is to leave no loose ends.'

'But he's leaving.'

'I said be quiet before I treat you as a loose end.'

For long minutes Nat sat in the bushes, the barrel pressed against his neck. Then further down the trail, a bush shook. Nat looked away from the bush, but Clifford tensed behind him, his hand slipping around Nat's mouth again.

'He don't know where we are,' Clifford muttered, 'but I know where he is.'

The cold steel on Nat's neck lifted and Nat tensed. From the corner of his eye, he saw the barrel swing round to the bush. Nat clubbed his hand up, knocking the gun.

Clifford's gunshot clattered wild.

With the back of his hand, Nat smashed Clifford across the jaw. Clifford stood straight with the blow. He staggered back and glared at Nat, his gun aiming down at him.

Unable to defend himself, Nat stared up.

Then a gunshot rang out and Nat gritted

his teeth, but Clifford tumbled over, a spreading redness across his chest.

Nat stood and stared down at Clifford, watching him squirm.

Spenser sauntered down the trail to them, his gun held out. When he reached the bushes, he snorted and shook his head.

'Looks like this is over,' Nat said.

'Yeah,' Spenser muttered, brandishing his gun towards Clifford. 'Seems like you got a dead man's choice, bounty hunter.'

'What's that?' Clifford muttered through gritted teeth.

'You can bleed to death or choose my way.'

Clifford rubbed a hand over his bleeding chest and spat to the side. 'And what's your way?'

Spenser grinned.

Clifford nodded and glanced away. Then he levered up his gun arm, the gun swinging towards Spenser.

Spenser fired two shots, Clifford rising and falling with each blast.

'Enough,' Nat shouted, grabbing Spenser's arm. 'He's dead.'

Spenser smiled and holstered his gun.

'Then this is really over.'

'Yeah.' Nat sighed. 'I was wrong before. I do understand how this works.'

They stared at Clifford's body and without discussion, they left it in the bushes. Then they rounded up Clifford's horse and packhorse. In silence, they slipped Kirk's body from the back. They dragged it to the side of the trail and threw it into the bushes beside Clifford's body.

Nat mounted his horse and stared at Kirk's body, shaking his head. 'Rory was right,' Nat said. 'He ain't looking like six thousand dollars.'

Spenser nodded. 'Someone will find him and try to collect.'

Nat sighed. 'And they'll fall out and kill before they get that bounty.'

'Yeah,' Spenser said. 'Don't matter to me. I ain't collecting on my former boss, but I don't understand your reason.'

Nat shrugged. 'I reckon you do.'

'Perhaps.' Spenser mounted his horse and stood on the trail, a light breeze ruffling his clothes. 'So you ain't returning to Beaver Ridge?'

'Nope. There's nothing for me there.' Nat swung his horse round to Spenser's side. 'Where you heading?'

'West.'

Nat sighed. 'West sounds good, if you don't mind company.'

With a returning nod, Spenser pulled on his reins and the two men rode west, heading into the lowering sun.

At the top of the first ridge, Nat stopped and glanced back.

Further down the trail, some of Harmony's townsfolk had ventured from the town and stood over Clifford and Kirk's bodies. They pushed and shoved each other in their eagerness to get hold of Kirk's body.

With a shake of his head, Nat pulled on the reins, turning his horse, and hurried after Spenser.

The publishers hope that this book has given you enjoyable reading. Large Print Books are especially designed to be as easy to see and hold as possible. If you wish a complete list of our books please ask at your local library or write directly to: